P9-BYO-721

A PORTRAIT OF LOVE

He seemed to fill the whole room, the sky, and the world itself, and she knew as she saw his eyes that he looked younger and happier then and completely different from the man she had left behind.

Neither of them could speak, they just stood looking at each other. Then the Earl opened his arms and with a little cry that seemed to echo round the room Fedora ran towards him.

He held her close against him and she could feel his heart beating frantically against her breast.

Then he turned her face up to his and looked down at her before his lips were on hers.

He kissed her until the whole room swung round them, and they no longer had their feet on the ground but were flying towards the Heaven they had sought before and lost.

A Portrait
of
Love

Barbara Cartland

A Portrait of Love

First Published in United States 1981
ⓒ 1981 Barbara Cartland
This Edition Published by **Book Essentials South** 1999
Distributed by **BMI**, Ivyland, PA 18974
PRINTED IN THE UNITED STATES OF AMERICA
ISBN 1-57723-424-3

Author's Note

Many of the magnificent collections of paintings in the ancestral homes of Great Britain are, fortunately, still intact. My son-in-law, the Earl Spencer, has at Althorp in Northamptonshire one of the finest collections in the country.

He possesses twenty Van Dycks so beautiful that one is entranced by the artist's technical brilliance and psychological insight. Born in 1599, he died in 1641, but in that short time he produced hundreds of amazingly fine paintings.

Charles I settled on him an annual pension of two hundred pounds, presented him with two houses, and gave him a Knighthood. No artist deserved it more.

Chapter One

1841

Fedora was dusting the Sitting-Room when Jim came in through the door.

He was a small, wiry little man getting on in years, with his hair just turning grey over his ears. But he had the honest eyes that reminded her of the devotion of a spaniel.

" 'Tis no use, Miss Fedora," he said. " 'E won't let us 'ave any more food 'til we pays for it."

Fedora sighed.

It was what she had expected, but the only shop in the village had been exceedingly lenient over their account, which had risen higher and higher until she was ashamed to ask for even a loaf of bread.

"We shall have to sell something," she said, speaking more to herself than to Jim.

"I could take one of th' pictures up to London, Miss Fedora."

"We know we have no right to sell them," Fedora answered. "They belong to Mr. Philip, and what will he say when he comes home to find them gone?"

"I daresay as 'e won't think th' pictures important if you and th' Master be in yer graves," Jim said with unanswerable logic.

Fedora sighed again.

She had fought resolutely against selling the last assets

1

the house possessed while her brother was away in the East trying to make his fortune.

She had always thought that to part with the paintings that had been collected by generations of Colwyns all down the centuries would be like betraying her own blood.

The collection at Mountsorrel was famous and would have attracted more attention if they had ever entertained, which they could not afford to do.

It was difficult to understand how her father had managed to carry on for so long in the great house which had passed from father to son since the reign of Queen Elizabeth.

He had inherited a pile of debts which had been like a millstone round his neck, and it looked like it would continue to be the same for his only son.

The owner of Mountsorrel was fiercely proud of his heritage and would have continued to live at Mountsorrel if it had been nothing but a hole in the ground.

As it was, he and his daughter occupied only a few rooms in the great house, and in the rest the ceilings fell down, the rats crept out of the wainscoting, the badly fitting windows let in the rain, and the holes in the roof grew larger year by year.

And yet, in the rooms they occupied, where there were threadbare carpets, curtains that were nothing but rags, and chairs which were in such a bad state of repair that it was difficult to sit on them in any comfort, there were paintings on the walls worth a fortune.

They were, of course, entailed onto Philip and after him his sons and grandsons and the future generations which would follow.

If there were Trustees to see that the paintings were kept intact, Fedora had never heard of them, and she fancied that if they had ever existed, most of them must now be dead.

But there was no need for Trustees or Guardians to preserve what every Colwyn thought of as something so precious that in the past they had died to preserve it and were prepared to do so again.

Looking round the walls, she thought it was astounding to see paintings that any Museum would have pleaded on their knees to possess.

There was a Holbein which portrayed the artist's uncannily shrewd insight into human nature, and the colours in his unique style seemed to blend in a remarkable way with those of the Hogarth hanging next to it.

Because she knew she could not bear to part with either of these, Fedora looked at a lovely Fragonard in which her father had told her realism and abstraction achieved a uniquely even balance.

It was a painting which Alexander Colwyn would often stand looking at for a long time, and she knew that whatever else was sold she could not deprive him of that.

Instead, she hesitated in front of a Raeburn. It was conspicuous with its vigorous modelling, its robust colouring, and, as her father had said so often, its understanding of character.

"What an artist!" he had exclaimed only the previous week. "And he made no sketches but painted straight onto a canvass."

There was despair in Fedora's large eyes as she turned from the Raeburn to a Van Dyck that showed in his inimitable manner an owner of Mountsorrel with the house behind him, his hat on his head, a stick in his hand, as if he was about to walk through the gardens to inspect some part of his Estate.

But she knew as she looked at them that whatever else went, the family portraits must remain intact, and she said again, as if she was speaking to herself rather than to Jim, who was beside her:

"We must not touch anything in this room."

"There's a number piled against the wall next door."

Fedora gave a little cry.

"Papa is working on those. He would be aware immediately if one was missing."

3

It would have struck a stranger entering the house that in the otherwise shabby, dilapidated building, every painting on the wall shone with the brilliance of a polished jewel.

It was as a comparatively young man that Alexander Colwyn came into his sadly depleted inheritance, and he decided he must do something about the paintings.

Because they had been neglected both by his father and his grandfather, despite the fact that they had been very proud of them, some were bulging from their frames, others had paint peeling off them, and every one had darkened with age, so that the original colour and beauty were obscured.

Alexander Colwyn when he was at Oxford had made friends with a man who had inherited a great house and a magnificent collection of paintings besides a respected title.

He had also inherited enough money with which to keep his treasures in the style they deserved.

Alexander Colwyn had stayed with him on several occasions and had learnt who was the best restorer in the country to work on his paintings so that they should look as they had when they had first left the artist's Studio.

On finding out who the man was, Alexander Colwyn had not only called to see him in London but had persuaded him to accept him as a pupil, to learn a skill in which he found there were few men who were really proficient.

When he returned home he started on his own paintings, working on them one by one until he had restored them to their original perfection.

What had started as a necessity became a joy and an interest which was more than a hobby—indeed, as Fedora sometimes teased him, it was almost a professional career.

Many of his friends begged Alexander's help for their own collections and he was only too pleased to oblige them.

It was Fedora who thought bitterly, as her father was thanked but obviously expected no payment for his services, that to buy the materials necessary for the restoration of rich men's treasures they had to go without food.

In the last year, however, Alexander Colwyn had not been well and had been obliged to refuse to work for both friends and acquaintances.

Because he had taught Fedora his skill and relied on her to help him, she had sometimes wondered if she should reply to enquiries that they would treat the paintings provided that they were paid for their work.

But she knew that her father would be horrified at the idea, and that it would upset him so much that it was not worth even suggesting it, for he would consider it an humiliation.

But now they had come to the end of the road, and unless some way of obtaining money was found, her father would die.

She was well aware that it was not only an obscure illness which was retarding his recovery, but the fact that he was under-nourished, and it was impossible for her to buy the food that the Doctor considered necessary.

When Philip was at home he had shot rabbits on the Estate, and ducks when they flighted down on the stream which ran through the ancient Park into what had once been a beautiful lake.

It was now neglected and overgrown with weeds, irises, and water-lilies, which had multiplied until they nearly covered the surface of it.

But Philip was not there, Jim was not handy with a gun, and anyway they could not afford the cartridges.

They kept hens, which provided them with eggs, but when they ate those who grew too old to lay, it was difficult to replace them.

The vegetables which Jim planted when he had the time were not very sustaining for a man who was ordered meat by the Doctor and every other sort of nourishing fare.

"We will look upstairs, Jim," Fedora said. "There is a

Fra Filippo Lippi in my room. Perhaps Papa will not be aware of it."

As she spoke, she knew that to lose the exquisite painting of the Virgin adoring the Child would be like losing a part of herself.

Fedora had gazed so often at the delicacy of Lippi's work, his sense of colour and the mysticism and spirit of contemplation shown on the painting, that she knew it had truly become a part of her mind.

The only alternative was another painting that she had made peculiarly her own, and this for an even more personal reason.

In her bedroom, to which she had moved it after her mother's death, was *A Rest on the Flight from Egypt* by Van Dyck.

Her father had always said that the Madonna holding the Holy Baby against her breast resembled the girl he had married, and her mother had always accepted the compliment because there was an undoubted likeness.

As Fedora grew older she had said:

"It may be like me, my darling, but really it might be an actual portrait of you."

Fedora had been so thrilled by the idea that she had gazed at the painting until she felt that even if the likeness had not been there before, the Madonna's face had gradually been imprinted on hers.

She also had soft dark hair over an oval forehead, a pointed little face, a straight nose, and large innocent eyes.

So she saw not only herself when she looked at her reflection in the mirror but also the face of the Madonna.

"How can I let that go?" she asked now.

Because it hurt her so intensely to think of parting with anything so beautiful, she walked to the window to stand looking out onto the untidy tangled bushes which, untended by gardeners, had grown into a jungle, beautiful, wild, and primitive.

" 'Tis no use, Miss," Jim said, behind her. "We've got to do somethin', an' that's a fact!"

"I know, Jim, and I am ashamed that you should suffer with us. I am well aware that we should not know what to do without you."

As she spoke, she thought that Jim had not been paid any wages for at least a year and if she was hungry he was too.

They both ate as little as possible so that her father could have more to prevent him from losing his very frail hold on life.

"I will make a decision tonight," Fedora said firmly, "and when Papa has gone to sleep we will pack up whatever painting we have decided to sell and take it to Mr. Lewenstein in London. I know he will give us a fair price."

Mr. Lewenstein had often in the past begged her father to accept a fee for restoring some of the paintings he sold in his Gallery in Bond Street.

But Alexander Colwyn had lifted his chin high and told him he could keep his money and his paintings, and he was lucky he did not have to pay to look at the Mountsorrel collection.

"I am perfectly prepared to do so," Mr. Lewenstein had replied, "although the proper charge for such a privilege would be beyond my pocket."

Looking back now, Fedora wondered bitterly whether pride in such circumstances was not in itself false, because it made other people suffer.

Jim went from the Sitting-Room, and she knew he had gone to the kitchen and wondered what he could possibly concoct for her father's supper.

Because it was early summer there would be a few young vegetables in the garden, if they had not eaten them already, and perhaps because the weather had been warm and clement the hens would have laid better than they did in the cold.

When she looked at her father's blue-veined hands

hanging limply over the arms of the chair in which he was sitting, she knew that what he needed was something substantial to put, as the Doctor had said, "good red blood in him."

'Jim is right,' she thought, 'there is no use preserving the paintings for Philip if when he comes home from India, or wherever he is now, he finds that Papa and I have died of starvation!'

Last month he had sent them a few pounds, which had been extremely welcome, but they had been a mere drop in the ocean compared to what they owed in the village and what they needed in the way of seeds to plant in the garden and feed for the chickens.

"I think it will have to be the Jordaens," Fedora decided, thinking of the magnificent painting of Meleager and Atalanta which was hung on the stairs.

It had always been a joy to come into the house on a dark day and see the flaming colours which were characteristic of the greatest Flemish painter of the Seventeenth Century.

It would be better to part with that than the Rubens, and perhaps she could keep from her father the knowledge that it was sold by merely saying that the walls were damp and she had put it in a safer place.

He was so tired and so limp these days that she had the feeling that he would not question her decision too closely.

"The Jordaens must go," Fedora decided, "and perhaps one day, if Philip makes his fortune, he will be able to buy it back."

It was a forlorn hope, but nevertheless it was better to be optimistic than to accept that it would be lost to the Mountsorrel collection forever.

As if she realised she was wasting her time instead of doing the innumerable tasks awaiting her in the house, Fedora continued with her dusting.

As she did so, she knew that what the furniture needed was polish, only she could not afford to buy the ingredients with which to make it.

She had just finished the mantelpiece when she heard a knock on the front door.

She wondered who it could be and thought that if Jim was in the kitchen he would be unlikely to hear it.

Putting down her duster, she left the room which, when the Drawing-Room had been in use, had been known as the Morning-Room, and walked into the Hall.

In her grandfather's time this had been very impressive with its marble floor, its carved staircase sweeping up to a landing on the First Floor, and the diamond-paned windows rising on either side of the front door to a painted wooden ceiling.

Now it looked faded and sadly in need of paint, and only the paintings on the wall glowed like gems that were badly set.

Fedora opened the door.

The postman was outside, an elderly man who carried on with his job despite the fact that he had a twisted leg.

"Good-day Miss Colwyn! Oi've brought a letter for ye."

"Thank you," Fedora replied. "And how is your wife? I hope she is feeling better."

"Her be a perkin' up a bit, Miss, with th' warm weather, an' so be th' children."

"I am glad to hear it," Fedora said.

She took the letter from him and he touched his cap as he limped away, carrying his satchel that contained the letters under his left arm.

'Another bill, I expect,' Fedora thought despondently.

They still occasionally had letters from London asking if there was any chance of the debts incurred by her father years ago, and his father before that, being paid.

Because the answer was always the same, most of the tradesmen had either given up and written them off as a bad debt, or else had died in the process of collecting.

Then as Fedora glanced down at the envelope, she saw that it was certainly not a bill. It was of thick, expensive parchment and was sealed and stamped with a crest which looked impressive.

It was addressed to her father, and whoever had inscribed it had obviously not known him well, for he had merely written: *"Mr. Colwyn"* above the address.

Fedora had no conscience about taking the letter into the Sitting-Room and slitting it open.

She had decided months ago that her father should not be disturbed or worried by anything except his ill health.

She took the greatest care in telling him only things that would please him.

From inside the envelope she drew a piece of writing-paper which was also of thick, expensive quality, and when she opened it she saw that there was an elaborate crest above the address.

Because she was curious, she read first what was written in a neat, copper-plate writing by what she thought was a secretary or a superior clerk.

> *"It has been brought to the notice of the most noble the Earl of Heversham that you are an expert in restoring pictures, and you have been highly recommended to His Lordship.*
>
> *You must have heard of the very fine collection of pictures which are hung at Heversham Castle, and, with the exception of those in the Royal establishments, they are considered to be the finest in the country.*
>
> *His Lordship therefore invites you to come to Heversham Castle as soon as possible to restore some of the pictures that are in need of it and varnish a number of others.*
>
> *Your usual fee for the work will of course be acceptable to His Lordship, and I should be grateful if you would notify me by return mail when we may expect you to start.*
>
> *Yours respectfully,*
> *Ebenezer Jenkins,*
> *Secretary to His Lordship*

As she finished reading, Fedora gave a little gasp.

She had been brought up in the history of Art since she was old enough to think, and she would not have been her father's daughter without being aware that the

Heversham collection was of great repute and extolled by every connoisseur.

In fact, Mr. Lewenstein had often compared the paintings at Mountsorrel with those owned by the Earl of Heversham.

"He's got more Van Dycks than you, Mr. Colwyn," Fedora had heard him say to her father, "but there isn't one to equal the Van Dyck painting of your ancestor. The smile on that face, which is definitely that of a Don Juan, has a brilliance that I've never seen in any other of his paintings."

Mr. Lewenstein had said very much the same about a Rembrandt that hung in her father's bedroom, at which he looked first thing every morning and last thing every night.

"There are several Rembrandts in the Heversham collection, Mr. Colwyn," he had said, "but if I had my choice, I would rather own yours than all those belonging to the Earl!"

Nevertheless, Fedora thought it would be very exciting to see other works by the artist whose painting she had known ever since she was a baby.

Then as she looked down again at the letter in her hands, she knew there was no chance of her ever reaching Heversham Castle.

Not only was her father incapable of making the journey and of working, but also he would undoubtedly feel insulted at being written to in such a manner and treated by the Earl's secretary and the Earl himself as if he were a tradesman.

She gave a little sigh because it seemed such a marvellous opportunity to see the world outside Mountsorrel, which, although she would never have admitted it, had become in the last few years a prison, even though it was without bars.

Then suddenly she had an idea.

For the moment it seemed so outrageous that she thought she must be mad even to consider it.

Then as she thought it over she told herself that it was like a shaft of sunshine coming through the clouds, at a moment when she had decided she must break the entail and sell a painting which belonged not to her father or to Philip but to the Colwyns that had not yet been born.

With the letter still in her hand, she ran from the room down the passage towards the kitchen.

It took her some time to reach it because the house was so large.

In the kitchen there had once been a Cook and at least three kitchen-maids, aided by scullery-maids and dairy-maids.

Near it was the Pantry, where a Butler and four footmen would polish the silver, and there had been other men to do the odd jobs like carrying in the wood and the coal.

There had even been a knife-grinder in her grandfather's time, Fedora thought with a little smile, whose job had been to sharpen and clean the knives after every meal on a stone which still stood in an alcove in the passage.

But at the moment she was not looking back into the past but was intent on finding Jim.

He was bending over the ancient stove, which was kept working apparently by sheer willpower and what Fedora often thought was a magic touch. He was stirring something in a sauce-pan which, because she was hungry, smelt delicious.

However, this was not the moment to think of the rumblings of her stomach, which always preceded the frugal meals at which there was never enough to eat.

"Listen, Jim, to the letter I have just received," she said.

He turned to look at her, then continued stirring the contents of the sauce-pan, although she knew he was listening.

She read him the letter, and when she had finished Jim laughed laconically.

"Th' Master won't like that! Impertinence, I calls it! And that be nothin' to wot 'e'll say!"

"I shall not show it to him," Fedora said quickly. "But, Jim, I have an idea!"

"An' wot might that be?"

"You will go to London tomorrow, as we agreed," Fedora answered, "but instead of a painting, you will take this letter to Mr. Lewenstein. You will ask him to lend us the money to get to Heversham Castle and also to buy enough food and medicines to make Papa well enough to travel."

Now Jim left the spoon in the sauce-pan and turned to look at Fedora with an expression of surprise on his face.

"You will promise him," she went on, "that we will pay him back as soon as we receive payment for restoring the paintings at Heversham Castle."

"The Master won't take no money, Miss Fedora, you knows that," Jim replied. "And what's more, he bain't well enough to do no work."

"No, of course he is not," Fedora agreed, "but I can do it for him. If they give us a room in which to work, there is no reason for them to know who is doing the actual restoring."

She saw by the expression in Jim's eyes that he understood what she was saying, and she went on:

"As for Papa receiving payment, which we know he will never accept, I will speak to the Earl myself and explain the position. I am sure he will understand. Anyway, when he sees Papa he will know he is a gentleman."

"There's no doubt about that, Miss," Jim agreed.

"There is just a chance that we can pull it off," Fedora said. "But if we cannot do so, then you know as well as I do that we shall have to sell a painting, and that will break Philip's heart."

As she spoke, she knew that if Jim was not prepared to agree with her, that argument would certainly convince him.

Jim adored Philip in the same way that he adored her father and herself.

He had once said in an expansive moment:

" 'Tmay seem impertinent, Miss Fedora, but yer're me

13

family, that's wot yer are! Me mother died soon after I were born, and if I 'ad a father, no-one told me 'is name. But yer treats me as if I was a 'uman bein', an' I feels as though I belongs."

"That is what I want you to feel, Jim," Fedora had replied, "and you know how fond Mama was of you. In fact, you are quite right—you are one of the family, and I do not know what we would do without you!"

As she spoke, she thought that there was something misty in Jim's blue eyes, and hastily, because she felt embarrassed, she had said:

"I often think how very lucky I am to have three men to look after me: Papa, Philip, and you. What woman could ask for more?"

Jim had laughed.

"One day you'll find yer own man, Miss Fedora. Then you'll have no use fer us."

As Fedora told him he was talking nonsense, the sentimental moment passed.

Jim was as intensely proud of Philip as if he were his own son, and when he had set off into the unknown, believing it was his only chance of making enough money for what was left of his family and for Mountsorrel, it was Jim who had choked back his tears.

Fedora had remained composed until the Stage-Coach which was carrying her beloved brother to Tilbury had disappeared out of sight in a cloud of dust.

Philip had written intermittently in the next two years, but for the last six months they had not heard from him.

"Perhaps he is on his way home," Fedora said to cheer up her father, who missed him.

But she could not help feeling afraid in case he was ill or in danger, or had spent the last of the money he had taken with him and had no idea where he could find more.

Sometimes she tortured herself by thinking that she would never see Philip again. Then she felt confident that her prayers would be heard and one day he would come back to them.

But now her only concern must be for her father, and both she and Jim were aware that he was growing weaker and weaker all the time.

"I'll go t' London and do as yer say," Jim said in a voice that showed he had made up his mind, "an' I'll make sure, Miss Fedora, that Mr. Lewenstein lends us enough money for all we needs. If the Master's staying at Heversham Castle, 'e must 'ave some new shirts. Them 'e's wearin' now ain't nothin' but rags!"

Fedora gave a little cry of protest.

"We cannot afford it, Jim! You know as well as I do that we cannot spend money on anything but necessities."

"Just two shirts, Miss Fedora," Jim said pleadingly. "I can wash one every night and 'ave the other aired and fresh for the mornin'. An' wot's more, if yer're stayin' in a grand place like that, the Master'll need 'is evenin'-clothes, so I'd better be gettin' them out an' cleanin' 'em up a bit."

"At least they should fit him," Fedora said beneath her breath.

She knew that because her father was so thin from lack of food, he would be able to wear any of the clothes that Jim had put carefully away in the wardrobe of the big Master Bedroom where for three hundred years the heads of the Colwyn family had slept.

"There's always a pot o' gold at th' end o' th' rainbow!" Jim said.

Because it was the sort of thing he said when she least expected it, Fedora laughed, and the sound seemed to ring out in the ancient kitchen.

Then, even as she laughed, she remembered that if her father needed new clothes, so did she.

"And that is certainly something we cannot afford!" she told herself.

She put the thought from her mind and, picking up the letter she had put down on the kitchen-table, said to Jim:

"You had better kill a chicken before you go to bed so that I can pluck it tomorrow and start feeding Papa with nourishing food even before you come back with the money."

"Ye can bet I'll be doin' that, Miss Fedora!" Jim replied.

There was a note of optimism in his voice which Fedora knew had not been there before, and it lifted her own spirits.

What she must hope was that this would be a piece of good fortune which would sweep away her anxiety about her father and the paintings for at least a little while.

What was more, from her own point of view it would be an adventure which she had never anticipated.

"The Heversham collection!"

She felt as if a new excitement was quickening her blood.

As she reached the Hall she could still hear far away at the end of the long corridor Jim whistling in the kitchen, and the sound reminded her of a will-o'-the-wisp enticing her over quagmires and quicksands to an imaginary land of strange delights.

She suddenly wanted, if not to whistle, to sing, and as she looked up at the paintings on the stairs she felt that they were smiling at her.

"For the moment," she said to them, "I have saved you from leaving us."

Then she imagined that they laughed, as she did, out of sheer delight.

* * *

The following morning, after a night in which she was too excited to sleep, Fedora saw Jim off to London.

He was carrying the letter from Heversham Castle in his inside pocket, and in another was Mr. Lewenstein's address in Bond Street, clearly written by Fedora.

They calculated that if he left by the first Stage-Coach, which passed the end of the village at six o'clock in the morning, he would be in London by luncheon-time and be able to catch the coach which came back the same way at about six o'clock in the evening.

It would be a long day, but Jim was used to working

long hours, and he knew that as Fedora would be anxious to hear the result of his visit, he must, if it was humanly possible, return that evening.

"I shall not tell Papa where you have gone," Fedora said. "Yet, because he is so perceptive, he already asked me this morning if in my dreams I had been left a fortune!"

"That's 'cos yer're looking 'appy, Miss Fedora," Jim said, "much happier than I've seen yer in a long time."

"It is because I feel that this is like a miracle when we have been so worried and . . . hungry," Fedora replied.

They both laughed because there had been so many days recently when they had looked despondently at what there was to eat and wondered how long they could last on such short-commons.

If Jim had not been skilful enough to catch some small fish in the stream, or snare a rabbit regardless of what the season was, things would have been worse.

But it was her father's health which worried Fedora so intensely, and at times she felt that she was being ridiculous not to sell even one painting which would keep them going for a year or so, rather than struggle on, trying to bow to tradition rather than to sheer necessity.

Then, as if in answer to a prayer, the letter from Heversham Castle had opened a new horizon.

What did it matter if the secretary addressed her father as if he were an ordinary tradesman, and what was the point of being blue-blooded and a gentleman if he died of starvation?

When Jim had left, having obtained the seat he wanted just beside the coachman and waved her a cheery smile as the coach drove off, Fedora walked back to the Manor.

Everybody seemed to be about in the village to bid her "good-morning" and ask after her father. Then one of the women in the cottages ran out with a loaf of bread in her hand.

"I've just bin bakin', Miss Fedora," she said, "an' I thinks p'raps your father would fancy a slice for his breakfast."

"How kind of you, Mrs. Coles," Fedora replied. "I know how much he will enjoy it, for there is nobody in the whole village who bakes bread as well as you do."

"That's just wot your dear mother used to say," Mrs. Coles replied, "an' you're very like her, m'dear."

"Thank you," Fedora said, and carrying the loaf under her arm she walked on.

That she was not too proud to accept the loaf from Mrs. Coles created a generous impulse on the part of those who lived in the other cottages.

By the time she reached home she was carrying two very special brown eggs, which she had been told were far more nourishing than white ones, a pot of gooseberry jam that had been made the previous day, and a small pat of butter that had just come from the churn.

She was extremely grateful for what she was given and was touched by the kindness of the villagers.

At the same time, she knew that her father would be horrified if he realised that the whole village was aware that they could no longer obtain credit from the local shop.

Hoping that he would not ask awkward questions, Fedora boiled the eggs for his breakfast, spread butter on the bread, and put the pot of gooseberry jam on his tray.

She thought, or she may have imagined it, that when she went back later there was a little more colour in his pale face, and his eyes seemed more sparkling and alive than they had been earlier in the morning.

"I enjoyed my breakfast, Fedora," he said simply. "Tell Jim the bread is far better than what he has been baking lately. He must try to keep up his standard."

"I will tell him that, Papa," Fedora replied, taking the tray from his bedside.

She knew as she walked downstairs that the reason why Mrs. Coles's bread was so much more enjoyable was that Jim was forced to use the cheapest possible flour and inferior yeast.

As he might have said himself: "Yer can't make bricks without straw!"

Her thoughts were with Jim, travelling to London, and she almost wished she had gone herself. It would have been an adventure!

'I have not set foot out of Mountsorrel for at least twelve months,' she thought. 'Now, once Jim returns, we are going to Heversham Castle!'

She thought for some time before she picked up her pen to answer the letter she had received yesterday.

She decided that for her father's sake she must try to make the Earl understand who he was.

At the same time, she did not wish to say anything which might appear presumptuous.

Finally she wrote:

> *On the instructions of Mr. Alexander Colwyn of Mount-*
> *sorrel, I am empowered to thank you for His Lordship's*
> *invitation to visit Heversham Castle and inspect the paint-*
> *ings.*
>
> *As His Lordship's request indicates that the matter is*
> *urgent, Mr. Colwyn will arrange to come to the Castle next*
> *Wednesday, the Seventeenth of June, and I will inform His*
> *Lordship of the time the Stage-Coach will reach the nearest*
> *stop on the evening of that date.*
>
> *Mr. Colwyn will be accompanied by his daughter, Miss*
> *Fedora Colwyn, and his valet.*
>
> *Again on Mr. Colwyn's instructions, I ask you to thank*
> *His Lordship for the invitation and beg to remain His*
> *Lordship's Most Obedient and Respectful Servant,*
>
> *Adolphus Nicholson,*
> *Secretary*

Fedora could only smile as she signed the fictitious name with a flourish.

Then as she read the letter over she was rather proud of it.

'At least,' she thought, 'I shall give the Earl something to think about.'

She hoped he would be impressed.

Then she addressed the envelope in her well-formed and elegant handwriting that showed a great deal of character in it and took it down to the village Post-Office.

As she handed the letter in, she knew that the address would be read and reread before it was despatched, and in a short time the whole village would be aware that her father was communicating with the Earl of Heversham.

She stopped on her way back to the Manor to tell Mrs. Coles how much her father had enjoyed her newly baked bread, and said the same to the other women who had contributed to his breakfast.

Then as she stepped in through the front door, she remembered that as soon as Jim returned he would have to get down their trunks from the attics, where she was quite certain they would be thick with dust, although she hoped the rats had not been able to gnaw through the leather from which they were made.

Then it struck her that sometime after her mother's death she had packed away all her clothes.

It was then, for the first time since the Earl's letter had arrived, that Fedora was vividly aware of her own appearance.

If her father required new shirts, it was nothing to what she needed, and she knew without being told that her clothes were a disgrace.

For one moment she panicked.

She had been so intent on thinking of the paintings at Heversham Castle that she had forgotten there would be people there too, and now she knew she would be ashamed for them to see her.

It was a pity, she thought cynically, that she could not dress herself in one of their Van Dycks, drape a Rembrandt over her shoulders, and use the Fragonard as a skirt.

But as that was impossible, she would have to appear in her rags, and if the occupants of Heversham Castle did not like it, they would just have to look the other way.

"I will do my best with Mama's clothes," she told herself, "but they were old and worn when she died."

She looked up at the Jordaens on the stairs, and she

wished she could take from the painting the alluring gown
Atalanta was wearing.

She thought too that the blue robes of the Virgin in
the *Fra* Filippo Lippi in her bedroom would be very
effective as a wrap if it was cold in the evening.

Jim had said that her father would need evening-
dress, but what was she to wear?

Without even looking, she knew there was nothing
possible in her empty wardrobe.

Then she was running as quickly as she could up the
stairs, through the Hall, up again to the Second Floor,
and she was breathless when she finally reached the
attics.

She moved along the dusty, uncarpeted floor towards
the box-room, and as she went she was praying, almost
like a child might do, to her mother:

"Help me, Mama, help me! I need a miracle—or rather an evening-gown!"

Chapter Two

Fedora was sewing in the Sitting-Room when she heard footsteps in the Hall and knew that Jim must have returned.

Before she could jump to her feet, he had opened the door and there was a triumphant grin on his face that told Fedora without words that he had been successful.

At the same time, she had to ask:

"Is everything all right, Jim? Mr. Lewenstein understood?"

" 'E were delighted, Miss Fedora," Jim replied, "and 'e gives me enough to stop us from worryin' at any rate fer a few months."

"How much?" Fedora asked automatically.

"Fifty pounds!"

Fedora's eyes widened, but it was impossible even to gasp as Jim went on:

"I explains to Mr. Lewenstein exactly what 'appened, an' tells him yer was thinking of coming to him with one o' yer pictures, an' 'e coughs up without a murmur."

"Oh, Jim, it is too much!" Fedora exclaimed.

"Don't yer believe it, Miss Fedora. I stops on my way back through the village an' pays 'em what was owed at th' shop. I thought yer'd want me to do that."

"Of course, Jim."

"And I buys everythin' that'll put the Master on 'is feet. I'm a-starting cookin' right away."

Even though Fedora thought she ought to expostulate

23

at changing one debt for another, she knew that Jim had been right to do what he had.

What was important was to get her father well and to arouse him from his lethargy with the excitement of visiting Heversham Castle.

She had not yet told him about the invitation because she was so afraid that Mr. Lewenstein might be away or refuse their request, in which case they would be unable to go.

"What's more, Miss Fedora," Jim went on, "Mr. Lewenstein says it'd be a great mistake for the Master, in 'is state of 'ealth, to attempt the journey in one day. 'E suggests you stay the night at 'is 'ouse in London and 'e'll find a carriage to take you to the Castle."

"Surely that would be very expensive," Fedora protested.

"Yer can leave that to Mr. Lewenstein," Jim said confidently, "and 'e's right, Miss Fedora. Yer don't want the Master to arrive in a state of collapse."

"No, of course not," Fedora said quickly.

"Well, it's all arranged," Jim said, "and we'll get the Master to London on Tuesday, and yer mark my words, by the time 'e's eaten and drunk all I've brought 'im, 'e'll be a different man!"

In the next two days Fedora began to think Jim was right.

The best cuts of beef, the tender veal, and the fat chickens which Jim provided seemed every hour to put new life into a man who was suffering from a form of starvation.

Over six foot and with a heavy frame, Alexander Colwyn had been strong all his life and was not in the least like so many dilettante painters who rather gloried in looking delicate and sensitive.

When he had fine horses he had been an outstanding rider, and Fedora could remember as a child that in the summer he would swim daily in the lake before it became so blocked with weeds.

It was only when they grew so poor and he was obliged to live on what he called "rabbit food" that he began to lose his strength. And after his wife died he lost interest in almost everything except his paintings.

At first, when Fedora told him they had been invited to Heversham Castle he stared at her incredulously.

"Did you say Heversham?" he enquired.

"Yes, Papa. We have often talked of the magnificent collection of paintings owned by the Earl of Heversham, and he is asking you to visit him and see them."

"Why?"

"Because he wants your advice," Fedora answered quickly, "and I suspect he will also want your help in restoring them."

To her relief, her father did not ask actually to see the letter that contained the invitation.

She was quite certain that if he did so, he would feel insulted and would refuse categorically to go to Heversham Castle.

He was, however, so intrigued by the invitation that he responded almost eagerly to her insistence that he must get well enough to travel, and the best way to do that was to eat everything that Jim provided.

Jim also bought him the medicine which the Doctor had prescribed some months previously but which, after the first bottle, they had found was too expensive.

On the Monday after Jim's return from London, her father was walking round the house inspecting his own paintings, and Fedora knew he was calculating how they would compare with the Heversham collection.

"Of one thing you may be quite certain," her father said, "he will not have a Van Dyck to rival the one hanging in your bedroom."

He said this when he was standing looking at the exquisite face of the Madonna, and by the expression in his eyes Fedora knew he was thinking that it resembled her mother.

Because she knew it would please him, she slipped her hand into his and said:

"I do not think either of us, Papa, need feel humbled by what we shall see at Heversham Castle. The Earl may beat us in quantity, but I am quite certain that when it comes to quality there is no-one who has a better collection than you."

Her father smiled.

"That is what I would like to think," he said, "but I do not mind telling you, my dear, that I shall be extremely annoyed if I am wrong!"

They both laughed.

Then Fedora begged her father to rest and not over-tax his strength before the journey on the following day.

She also wished to put the last finishing touches to her gowns before she packed them.

She was well aware how inadequate they were, and even with the addition of her mother's wardrobe she knew that she would look old-fashioned and very shabby.

Then she cheered herself up by thinking that the Earl of Heversham was an old man and perhaps there would be no other guests at the Castle except for themselves.

She wished she knew more about him, and then she thought that that was information which Mr. Lewenstein might easily be able to impart.

On the question of clothes, she was determined that not one penny of the money they had borrowed from the Art-Dealer should be expended on anything but their debts and on food for her father.

It was Jim who insisted that she should eat the same things, only in smaller amounts.

"Yer've got to be well too, Miss Fedora," he said firmly, "and I'm not cooking just one slice of anything I buys."

Fedora knew he was talking sense, and what was more, if she had been on short-commons these last months, so had Jim.

They ate better than they had for a very long time, and the worries that had rested on her shoulders like a heavy burden seemed to lighten. When she heard Jim whistling as he worked, she wanted to sing.

Besides her own clothes there were her father's to be packed, and while Jim had sponged and pressed everything he could, Fedora darned her father's socks, sewed on buttons, and with minute stitches mended his underwear.

Jim had brought back from London two new shirts that had stiff collars and a wide black cravat for her father's neck.

When he was dressed, Alexander Colwyn certainly looked extremely distinguished.

If his coat was cut in a slightly old-fashioned way, and his tall hat had seen better days, he looked every inch the gentleman he was and exactly as the owner of Mountsorrel should look.

Because she and Jim had been so busy, Fedora did not feel the excitement of it all until they were waiting on the main road for the Stage-Coach.

Because the whole village was aware of where they were going, her father had not had to walk from his house to the village, since the Vicar had kindly collected them in his Chaise.

It was an ancient vehicle in which he travelled round the furthest parts of his Parish, and he conveyed them and their luggage in it to the stop where the Stage-Coach set down one lot of passengers and collected others.

"This is very kind of you, Reverend," Alexander Colwyn said.

"It is nice to see you about again, Mr. Colwyn," the Vicar replied, "and it is a great honour that the Earl of Heversham should turn to you for assistance."

Fedora, listening to the conversation, stiffened when she heard the Vicar say the word "assistance," and she hoped that her father had not noticed it.

"I have always wanted to see the Heversham collection," he remarked, "and I am greatly looking forward to the experience."

"I envy you," the Vicar said. "I often think how fortunate it is that we who live in Little Sorrel have the privilege of seeing your paintings."

It was not surprising that by the time her father got into the Stage-Coach he was in an exceedingly good humour, and Fedora thanked the Vicar effusively for his kindness.

"Now you take care of your father, Miss Fedora," the Vicar replied, "and bring him home safely. We are very proud of him in Little Sorrel."

As he saw the expression of gratitude in her eyes, he thought that she was the loveliest girl he had ever seen in his life. It was a pity that she was not better dressed for such an expedition, but as he knew little about ladies' dress, he hoped he might be mistaken.

The Stage-Coach set off with Fedora and her father inside, with fortunately only two other occupants, and Jim perched up on his favourite seat beside the coachman.

It took a long time for them to reach London, with frequent stops and passengers getting in and out all the time, and by the time they drove into the courtyard of the Two-Headed Swan at Islington, Alexander Colwyn was very tired.

Jim found them a hackney-carriage and they drove off to Mr. Lewenstein's house in St. John's Wood.

It was not large, Fedora found, but very comfortable if rather ornately furnished.

But before she could spend time looking at anything, she realised it was most important that she should get her father into bed.

Mr. Lewenstein provided him with a brandy which swept away the worst of his fatigue, although once he was in bed he looked so pale that Fedora was worried.

"It has been too much for him," she said to Jim as they left her father's room to find their own rooms.

" 'E'll be all right, Miss, when I've brought 'im up somethin' better than they served at that Inn where we ate. It wasn't good enough for rats, let alone 'umans!"

Fedora had to smile. At the same time, she knew that Jim was speaking the truth.

Stage-Coach passengers, she had always heard, were catered for indifferently at country Inns, and the one at which they had stopped at midday was no exception.

As was to be expected, Mr. Lewenstein's food was excellent, but as over-rich as his house.

There was pâté, pigeons stuffed with succulent spices, beef garnished with oysters, besides half-a-dozen other dishes, each more exotic than the last.

"How can you eat such delicious food and be so thin?" Fedora asked Mr. Lewenstein.

He smiled.

"You haven't seen my wife, my dear. She is unfortunately away from home and will be very sad to have missed you, but I am afraid, owing perhaps to her excellent catering, that she weighs nearly eighteen stone!"

Mr. Lewenstein said it in such a comical way that Fedora laughed, and she thought to herself that she and her father were certainly moving from one extreme to the other, or perhaps from the ridiculous to the sublime.

Mr. Lewenstein's carpets seemed softer and had a deeper pile than Fedora had ever known, and as she found that getting into bed was like sinking into a cloud, she thought she would never want to scramble out of it.

Before she retired, she and her host had a serious talk.

"Your man told me," Mr. Lewenstein said, "that before the invitation came from Heversham Castle, you were thinking of selling one of your father's paintings."

"They are not my father's," Fedora said in a low voice. "They belong to Mountsorrel, but I was desperate and thought there was no other way of saving his life."

"If you had written to me, Miss Fedora, and asked me to come and see your father, I would have done so."

"Yes, I know," Fedora answered. "You have always been extremely kind, Mr. Lewenstein. At the same time, this invitation was like a miracle. In fact, it has saved me from doing what I know is wrong."

"It will certainly keep your father alive, and in the future you must never let things come to such a pass again."

"If only Philip would come home! I would not feel it was such a responsibility to take upon myself," Fedora murmured.

"I have met your brother only once," Mr. Lewenstein said, "and a very handsome young gentleman I thought him. I cannot believe that he would not be prepared to sacrifice one painting to save his own father."

"Yes, of course he would," Fedora agreed.

Even as she spoke, she knew it was not as simple as all that.

The collection of paintings which meant so much to her father had been added to over the centuries by the Colwyns, and for one of them to break it up now would seem treacherous and dishonourable in a way that no-one who was not part of the family would understand.

"If this happens again," Mr. Lewenstein was saying, "you must send for me. I will gladly come down and advise you which painting should be sold and get you the best possible price, which should certainly keep you in comfort for a great number of years."

Fedora was just about to give a cry and explain that the last thing she wanted was for him to come to Mountsorrel, for then her father would know what was happening.

Then she thought that at this moment when things were going well, there was no point to make difficulties which might never arise.

So she merely said quietly:

"I am very grateful, Mr. Lewenstein, and I know that we can rely on you. I promise that I would not think of doing anything in the way of selling a painting without first asking for your advice and assistance."

She knew by the expression on the Dealer's face that she had said exactly what he wanted to hear, and she remembered that she was already tied to him by the loan she had accepted without her father's knowledge and which would one day have to be repaid.

Yet, it was impossible not to sleep comfortably and in fact dreamlessly in the luxury which Fedora had never known before.

When she was awakened in the morning to find that her travelling-gown had been pressed for her by a very competent maid and she was called with China tea in an exquisite Crown Derby teapot, she thought with a little sigh that pride was not a very comfortable thing to live with.

Then she chided herself for being disloyal, and rose hurriedly to dress before she went into her father's room to see what sort of night he had passed.

"I slept like a child," he said as he was helped into his clothes by Jim.

"I can promise you one thing, Fedora," he went on. "I have no intention of leaving this house until I have seen Lewenstein's treasures. I have always suspected that he keeps some of the best paintings he had for himself, and buys them at knock-down prices!"

Fedora glanced quickly at the door to see that it was closed.

"Do be careful, Papa," she begged. "He might hear what you are saying and be offended. He has been very kind to us."

"Yes, yes, of course," Alexander Colwyn agreed. "But make no mistake, my dearest, Lewenstein is a good business-man, and remember that with his race business always comes first."

Fedora did not wish to think her father was right, but she could not help feeling that if they had not the Mountsorrel collection of paintings in the background, perhaps Mr. Lewenstein would not have been such a generous and hospitable host.

They were offered such a large breakfast that it was impossible, Fedora thought, to eat more than a tenth of what was on the table. Then her father sat in the Drawing-Room and Mr. Lewenstein brought paintings, china, objets d'art, and books into the room for him to see and admire.

They were all magnificent, many of them were unique, and Fedora enjoyed what she thought of as the "Peep-Show" as much as her father did.

It was nearly noon before Mr. Lewenstein admitted that he had no more to display.

Then they were served what he called a "light lunchéon" before the carriage was brought to the door.

As there had been an excellent claret as well as a vintage brandy for her father to drink with the delicious food, it was not surprising that once they set off after many expressions of goodwill, he fell asleep.

Jim had arranged a piece of luggage opposite his seat on which he could raise his legs, there were cushions behind his back, and long before they left the main traffic of London behind he was sleeping soundly.

Fedora had sent another letter to the secretary at Heversham Castle. As she did so, she thought that to arrive in a carriage was far more impressive than travelling by Stage-Coach.

"Papa is also very much more comfortable," she told herself.

Looking at him with deep affection as he slept, she thought how grateful she was to Mr. Lewenstein that so far he seemed none the worse after the long journey yesterday and a night spent in a strange house.

After the despair of last week, when she had felt as if she were encompassed by a fog of despondency with a future dark and without hope, it was like stepping into the sunshine.

"Thank You, thank You, God," she prayed, "and please let Papa be well enough to work, so that we can earn some money and never again be in the same state as we were before the invitation came from Heversham Castle."

She thought perhaps she had been rather stupid to have let things slide for so long.

But now she knew that she too felt better than she had felt for a long time, and that lack of food had left her indecisive and so unsure of herself that it was almost impossible to make a decision about anything.

Now that her father was better, he would be his old positive, autocratic self, and she knew that was what she had missed during his illness.

She had been used all her life to having him order her about. At the same time, she always knew that he was a tower of strength on which she could rely, and that he would never fail her or anyone else for that matter.

When he had been so ill it was like seeing a great oak crumbling in front of her, and she had no idea how to cope with life without him.

"In the future I have to be firm and determined," she said now, "and not allow things to drift."

She felt that if her mother had been there she would have been ashamed of her, and she told herself humbly that she would try to do better in the future and certainly be more decisive than she had been in the past.

The journey was a long one.

Although the horses which drew the carriage which Mr. Lewenstein had provided for them were fresh when they started off and full of stamina, they ran into unexpected showers of rain which made the roads muddy and certainly impeded their progress when they got farther out in the country.

Then there were lanes that were narrow and twisting and the horses not only had to go more slowly but, as the afternoon wore on, were obviously getting tired.

It was then that the coachman lost his way and it took them some time to get back on the right road.

They had little assistance from the local yokels who appeared to have no idea where Heversham Castle was, and rather than admit it they were prepared to send them in the wrong direction.

It was nearly half-past-seven and the sun was sinking when finally Fedora was aware that they had turned in at some impressive lodge-gates and were driving down an avenue of oak trees.

She put her hand on her father's arm.

"Wake up, Papa!" she said. "We have arrived!"

"What? What is the matter?" Alexander Colwyn asked in the irritated tone of a man coming back to reality from the land of dreams.

"We are at Heversham Castle, Papa! We will be there in a few minutes!"

"It is time we were," her father said, sitting up and pulling the lapels of his coat into place.

Fedora thought the same, but she was concerned with tidying the ribbons of her bonnet, smoothing her skirt, and hoping it was not too badly creased.

Then she told herself it was unlikely that anyone would notice what she was wearing anyway.

She wished she had an elegant silk pelisse to wear, as was the fashion, instead of a rather worn paisley shawl that had seen its best days.

Then, forgetting herself, she looked out the window to see the Castle ahead of her.

She had thought it would look as if it had once been a Norman Castle belonging to a Baron and had been built as a defence against the insurgence of the conquered Anglo Saxons.

If that was its history, it had certainly changed.

Too late Fedora remembered that because there had been so much to talk about to Mr. Lewenstein, she had forgotten to ask him about Heversham Castle or its owner.

Then she had the suspicion that perhaps he knew as little as they did.

She thought too that as Mr. Lewenstein would never have seen the Heversham paintings, he would not wish to talk too much of something which would have proclaimed his ignorance.

Now she could see that the front of the Castle at any rate was of Georgian origin, tremendously impressive, with Corinthian columns supporting a carved portico, and the wings on each side of the main block surmounted by domes which glinted in the evening sunset.

It was extremely beautiful, but awe-inspiring.

However, it was impossible to get a proper impression of the whole building before the horses came to a stop at the bottom of a flight of steps, and Fedora bent forward to take her father's tall hat from the seat opposite them and put it in his hand.

There was a short pause, and Jim climbed down from the coachman's box before the front door was opened and two footmen came running down the steps.

Alexander Colwyn stepped out first, followed by Fedora.

She was aware that her father flexed his muscles after sitting, or rather lying, for such a long time, before he walked up the stone steps, his back very straight, looking, she thought, exceedingly distinguished as he entered the Hall.

There were several other footmen on duty and a Butler who came forward, looking slightly perplexed before he said:

"May I ask your name, Sir?"

"I am Mr. Alexander Colwyn and you are expecting me."

The expression on the Butler's face cleared.

"Mr. Colwyn, of course! And you are concerned with the paintings. We were expecting you, but not so late."

Before her father could reply, the Butler turned to the footman nearest to him and said:

"Tell the carriage to go to the side-door, where it should have gone in the first place!"

Then in the same breath he said:

"If you will follow the footman, Mr. Colwyn, he will take you upstairs to your rooms. Dinner will be served to you as soon as you are ready for it."

It was, Fedora thought later, more the way the Butler spoke than what he actually said.

She was aware that her father, who had stiffened when he heard the remark about the carriage, was now looking at the Butler with an expression in his eyes that made her hold her breath.

"Is the Earl of Heversham here?" he asked, and the question seemed to ring round the Hall.

"Yes, but His Lordship is entertaining. He will doubtless see you tomorr—"

The Butler got no further.

"You will announce me immediately!"

The way her father spoke made the Butler look up at him in surprise.

He had already handed his tall hat and the light over-

35

coat he had been wearing to a flunkey, and now as he straightened up to his full height he looked the aristocrat he undoubtedly was.

"You heard me!" he said in a voice that once again seemed to ring out. "You will announce me as Mr. Alexander Colwyn of Mountsorrel, and Miss Fedora Colwyn!"

As he spoke he was aware of the sound of voices, and, without waiting for the Butler, he walked across the Hall.

For a moment the servant was almost too surprised to realise what was happening. Then, flustered because by this time Alexander Colwyn had almost reached a pair of double mahogany doors, he moved ahead of him.

The Butler opened one door, the footman hurried to open the other, and Alexander Colwyn, at his proudest and most arrogant, swept into what Fedora saw was a magnificent and very beautiful Salon.

She had the impression of two glittering crystal chandeliers, each alight with dozens of candles.

Then as she was aware that there was a group of people at the far end of the room, the Butler announced:

"Mr. Alexander Colwyn of Mountsorrel, M'Lord, and Miss Fedora Colwyn!"

There was a sudden silence and Fedora felt as if everything glittered dizzily and it was difficult to focus her eyes.

Then as her father moved slowly but relentlessly down the room, she was obliged to follow him.

After what she thought was a palpable hesitation which could only be one of surprise, a man detached himself from the group by the mantelpiece and came towards them.

He was as tall as her father, broad-shouldered, and to her astonishment he was a young man, where she had expected an old one.

He was handsome, and yet at the same time there was an expression on his face which for the moment she was too frightened to interpret.

She felt excessively embarrassed and humiliated that her father had forced himself upon the Earl, who obviously had expected them to retire to their own quarters and certainly not intrude on his private party.

Her father, however, with his chin held high, was equally obviously not in the least abashed, but only determined to put the whole situation into its proper perspective.

Before the Earl could greet them, Alexander Colwyn held out his hand:

"Good-evening, My Lord! I must apologise that my daughter and I are so late in arriving, but the roads are in a bad state owing to the recent rains and the coachman lost his way. Please accept our apologies, especially as we will make you late for dinner."

The inference in what her father said brought the colour to Fedora's cheeks.

Then she was aware that if her father could cope with an unusual situation, so, after his first hesitation, could the Earl.

"I am delighted to see you, Mr. Colwyn," he said, "and I am sorry your journey has been such an unpleasant one."

The two men shook hands, and Alexander Colwyn, still in command of the situation, said:

"Allow me to present my daughter."

Fedora looked at the Earl for the first time and she thought that his eyes, which were grey, were strangely penetrating.

He looked at her as if she surprised him, and she supposed unhappily that it was her appearance which was responsible for that.

She curtseyed, then shook hands, and the Earl said:

"You must both have a drink and meet my friends."

A footman appeared with glasses of champagne, and while her father accepted his with an ease as if from long experience, Fedora felt as if her hand trembled as she lifted the crystal glass from the gold tray.

Then the Earl was introducing them:

"Mr. Alexander Colwyn, Lady Sheelah Turvey, Miss Colwyn . . ."

Then followed a stream of names that somehow did not penetrate Fedora's mind.

All she was thinking was that she had never in her life seen anyone as beautiful and spectacular as Lady Sheelah.

Wearing a gown of emerald-green satin, her bare neck and shoulders ornamented with emeralds and diamonds that must have cost a King's ransom, she glittered, and the vivid red of her hair was echoed in her eyes, which had a definite tinge of green.

Her lips were crimson, her eye-lashes undoubtedly darkened with mascara, and Fedora felt she must be staring at her open-mouthed as she had never imagined anyone could look so vivid and so colourful.

"And now," the Earl was saying as he introduced the last gentleman, "I am sure, Mr. Colwyn, you and your daughter would like to wash and change. We are, unfortunately, a long way from London."

"We will be as quick as we can," Alexander Colwyn replied, "and once again, my apologies for any inconvenience we may have caused you."

"It is of no consequence," the Earl said lightly.

He walked to the door to say to the Butler, who was waiting outside:

"Show Mr. and Miss Colwyn to their rooms, Dawson, and see that they have every assistance they need. Inform Chef that dinner will of course be delayed."

There was no need to look at the expression on the Butler's face, Fedora thought, to know that it had never crossed anybody's mind before they arrived that they would be dining with the Earl and not by themselves.

As the Butler himself led them up the stairs to hand them over to the Housekeeper who was waiting at the top, she could not help feeling slightly amused.

Her father in his usual arrogant manner had swept the social barriers aside and made himself felt when it was least expected.

But there was no chance of speaking of it to him now, and as he went into the room where Jim was waiting and a footman was already helping unpack his trunk, the

Housekeeper showed her into the bedroom next door.

It was a charming room, but they had walked a long way to find it and Fedora guessed that it was in the older part of the Castle.

However, there was no time now to speculate or to ask questions, for as if by magic, housemaids appeared to start unpacking and find her only evening-gown, which had been her mother's.

It was of deep rose-pink silk which was the same colour as the robe worn by the Madonna in the Van Dyck painting.

But as the bodice had been what was now unfashionably high, Fedora had cut it down and added a bertha of Venetian lace which was worn and torn with age. Fedora had mended it in a dozen places, but she was afraid it might disintegrate if handled roughly.

However, it had survived the journey, and when she had washed quickly she felt as she put it on that if she was not fashionable, at least she would not disgrace her father.

The gown was not nearly full enough, having been in vogue at the beginning of the last reign. The very full skirts and the off-the-shoulder gowns which had been introduced by the young Queen and became her so well were a fashion which Fedora thought wistfully she would never be able to buy for herself.

This gown was a pale reflection of them—but, she added to herself, very pale.

She was aware that Lady Sheelah's skirts contained yards and yards of the green satin which made her waist look tiny in comparison.

Her bertha was embroidered with diamanté and added to the glitter of her jewels.

Fedora had nothing to put round her neck but a narrow piece of velvet, which she had found among her mother's things and which matched the pink of her gown.

It broke the long line of her neck and was tied with a small bow at the back, and she hoped it gave her a touch of elegance.

Then she thought with a wry little smile:

'Nobody will notice me when Lady Sheelah is there!' and she merely glanced at her reflection in the mirror to see that her hair was tidy.

It was parted in the centre of her oval forehead and she attempted no fashionable coiffure but merely swept it back and twisted it into a roll at the back of her head.

As she had so much hair and it was so long, it was almost a chignon, and she thought that one day she must try to contrive to make it look fashionable, but there was no time now.

She had found among her mother's things a pair of lace mittens and they again had to be carefully darned, and she hoped as she put them on that they would not suddenly fall into shreds at any rate until after dinner.

"I think you are ready now, Miss," said the maid who had been helping her.

It was then that Fedora suddenly felt frightened.

How could she go downstairs looking, she was well aware, old-fashioned and very insignificant beside the fantastic, breath-taking beauty of the Earl's guest?

Then she told herself that she was being conceited to think that it was of any importance to anyone how she appeared or even that she was here.

The only thing that mattered was that somehow her father had reached Heversham Castle, and, although he was unaware of it and he must never find out, he was to be paid for what he would do here.

'I have to see the Earl alone!' Fedora thought, and the idea frightened her more than anything else.

The maid had opened the door for her and she stepped out into the passage to find as she did so that her father was coming from the room next door.

"You are ready, Fedora!" he exclaimed. "That is good! I do not know about you, but I am extremely hungry!"

She realised that he was still keeping up his attitude of being completely at home and quite unimpressed by his surroundings.

He looked tired, but as she looked back into the bedroom she saw Jim put a decanter of brandy on top of the chest-of-drawers and knew that he had stimulated her father into a sense of well-being which would carry him through dinner, if nothing else.

He was walking downstairs with a buoyancy in his step, and now as if to make amends for his mistaken attitude on their arrival, the Butler hurried across the Hall to open the door for him.

"Mr. Colwyn of Mountsorrel!" he announced. "And Miss Fedora Colwyn!"

Fedora saw that the Earl's other guests were still at the far end of the room and they still had glasses of champagne in their hands. But Lady Sheelah was seated in an arm-chair, looking petulant, and when she looked at her Fedora thought unhappily that there was no doubt she was annoyed at the delay.

Then as they walked down the room Fedora saw that her father's look of distinction in his evening-clothes had not escaped the red-haired beauty, and it was only when she looked at her that there was an undoubted expression of contempt in her green eyes.

"You have been unprecedentedly quick!" the Earl was saying.

"It is amazing what records a man can achieve when he is hungry!" Alexander Colwyn replied.

"And apparently a woman as well!" the Earl added.

A servant would have brought her a glass of champagne, but the Earl took it from the tray and held it towards her.

"I think you have earned this," he said.

He was looking at her strangely and his eyes seemed a little more penetrating than they had on their arrival. Because they made her feel shy, Fedora looked down and her eye-lashes were dark against her pale cheeks.

She felt she ought to say something, but she was not certain what it should be. However, fortunately dinner was announced and Lady Sheelah rose from her chair.

"At last!" she said in a rather sharp tone. "I began to

think it would be breakfast-time before we had anything to eat!"

The man who was standing beside her laughed.

"Now, Sheelah, that is unfair!" he said. "You kept us all waiting last night and the night before. If anyone is unpunctual for meals, it is you!"

"Only because I am trying to make myself look beautiful for you all," Lady Sheelah pouted, but her red lips were smiling.

"There is no need for you to try," was the answer.

However, she did not wait for the compliment, but walked towards the Earl, only, to her surprise and irritation, to hear him say to Fedora:

"As this is your first visit to my Castle, Miss Colwyn, may I escort you into dinner?"

Fedora was still feeling shy in a manner that was unusual for her, but she let her fingers rest lightly on the Earl's arm as her mother had told her in the past was correct.

As if her father realised what Lady Sheelah was feeling, he said:

"As a new arrival, may I claim the privilege of taking in someone so beautiful that I feel she has stepped out from one of His Lordship's famous paintings."

"Thank you," Lady Sheelah replied, "that is what His Lordship should say, if he were not so exceedingly remiss about such things."

They walked from the Drawing-Room into the passage, on each side of which there were hung paintings that made Fedora long to stop and stare.

She knew that was something she could not do now, and instead she was concerned with telling herself she should stop being gauche and awkward and behave with the same ease and polish that her father was showing.

It was no use excusing herself by saying that it was the first time in her life that she had dined in such a grand house.

Her mother had told her often enough that to be shy

and self-conscious was boring and a sign that she was thinking of herself rather than of other people.

Accordingly, when they had walked a little way she said:

"I am so looking forward, My Lord, to seeing your collection of paintings."

"Are you telling me that you know as much about them as your father?" he asked.

She thought this was a test.

"I hope I do," she replied. "I have been brought up from the cradle to think of little else."

The Earl laughed.

"I must certainly test your knowledge tomorrow, and I am sure, if nothing else, you will admire my Van Dycks."

"My father is quite certain that they will not equal ours," Fedora replied.

She knew that what she had said surprised him.

Because he was still thinking of her father as a professional craftsman, he asked:

"You own a Van Dyck?"

"Three, as it happens," Fedora answered. "One, which he said was the best he had ever painted, is of the Colwyn of Mountsorrel of the time, one of another member of the family, and the other is the *Rest on the Flight from Egypt*."

For a moment the Earl stiffened. Then he said:

"I know the painting you mean, but yours is of course a copy."

"A copy?"

"The original, painted by Van Dyck, is here at the Castle!"

For a moment Fedora was too astonished to reply, and by the time she realised the full significance of what he had said, they had reached the Dining-Room.

It was enormous, with a finely carved marble mantelpiece and a number of windows. Between them in every available space were paintings that she was certain were all by famous and reputable artists.

At the same time, it was obvious that many of them would need restoration and had grown too dark with age to be seen clearly.

The table was covered with gold ornaments and huge candelabra, each bearing four candles.

The dinner-service was of Sèvres and the Waterford glass was of a particularly fine design.

Fedora was seated on the Earl's left and Lady Sheelah on his right.

On Her Ladyship's other side was her father, who immediately got into a discussion with the man on his right about the inadequacy of the National Gallery.

It had been her father's contention for a long time that if a painting was being sold privately and was of great aesthetic value, it should be bought by the Nation.

Lady Sheelah immediately began a *sotto-voce* conversation that was obviously very intimate with the Earl. Meanwhile, because she was looking about her wide-eyed, it took Fedora a minute or two to realise that the man on her other side was watching her with an amused expression on his face.

"Well?" he asked at last. "What do you think of it?"

"This room?" Fedora enquired. "I think it is something out of a dream."

"You must tell that to your host, he will be delighted!"

Fedora glanced at the Earl and saw he was listening to what Lady Sheelah was saying to him, and she said in a low voice:

"I was expecting him to be old, but I suppose his father is dead."

"Kimball inherited last year," her dinner-partner replied. "He has been deeply worried over the condition of the paintings. His father was over eighty when he died, and had let the whole place slide. That is why, having heard of your father's reputation, he sent for him!"

He obviously realised as he uttered the words "sent for" that it sounded rude, and he added quickly:

"I mean—invited your father to come here, and may I

44

add that I am very glad you have accepted the invitation!"

"Thank you," Fedora replied. "It is certainly something I did not expect to happen to me."

"You sound as if you have not stayed in such a large house before."

"Not . . . exactly, and it is therefore an . . . adventure."

"I was watching you just now looking round the room, and I thought you appeared rather like a child at a magic-lantern show."

"Yes, of course! That is what it is," Fedora said. "But not a magic-lantern, a full-scale drama."

"And do you fancy yourself as the heroine?" a voice asked in a somewhat cynical tone.

She started, because, intent on speaking to the man on her left, she had not realised that the Earl was listening.

"Of course not, My Lord," she replied quickly. "I am only a spectator and I would doubtless, unless I was your guest, be sitting in the Gallery."

The Earl laughed.

"I do not believe that for a moment. Not when you tell me you have a Van Dyck at home, even if it is one which is somewhat suspect."

Fedora looked at her father, then lowered her voice as she said:

"Please . . . please . . . My Lord . . . do not let my father hear you say that . . . and if it is . . . possible . . . could I, before you have any . . . intimate conversation with him . . . speak with you . . . alone?"

The Earl raised his eye-brows and she knew he was staring at her, thinking perhaps that he could not have heard her correctly.

Then as she looked at him pleadingly, desperately afraid that he might say something which her father would overhear, he said quietly:

"Of course! Leave it to me!"

Chapter Three

Fedora awoke and lay for some time thinking of last night and what a strange evening it had been.

The party had, as she had said, been like a theatrical drama unfolding itself before her eyes, while she was just a spectator.

Only when Lady Sheelah retired to the Drawing-Room and she followed did fantasy become reality.

As she rose to leave the Dining-Room table, Lady Sheelah said to the Earl:

"Do not be long, dearest. You know how incredibly bored I shall be without you."

He did not reply and she swept towards the door, giving the gentleman who opened it for her a flirtatious look from under her darkened eye-lashes before she left the room.

Feeling small and insignificant, Fedora followed her, taking at the same time the opportunity of looking at the paintings on either side of the broad corridor.

She thought she recognised most of them and realised that nearly all of them needed attention.

With a little lilt of her heart, she thought that it would mean that she and her father would have to stay for a long time at the Castle, which, if nothing else, with the good food and congenial company would improve his health.

She had not missed the fact that her father was enjoying himself at dinner.

He was also, she thought, making it very clear that while the paintings at Heversham Castle were famous, he also had a collection which any connoisseur of paintings would know had its place in the world of Art.

Lady Sheelah reached the Drawing-Room and walked immediately to a gilt-framed mirror.

She stared at her reflection for some minutes, then drew a small vanity-box from the reticule she carried with her and which matched the green of her gown.

She proceeded to powder her nose, then to apply a salve to her already crimson lips, while Fedora watched her wide-eyed.

She was well aware, for her mother had told her so, that Ladies in the Social World were not supposed to use cosmetics.

"Nevertheless," Mrs. Colwyn had said with a smile, "they do so secretly, and very discreetly."

"I have never seen you use them, Mama," Fedora had answered.

"You and I are so fortunate, dearest," her mother had said, "in that we have a white skin which defies the elements and needs little or no ornamentation."

Fedora, who had been young at the time, touched her skin with her fingers.

"Is it different from anybody else's, Mama?"

"I think it comes from some far-off Spanish ancestor on my side of the family," her mother had answered. "My father always told my mother that her skin was like a magnolia."

Fedora had clapped her small hands together.

"That is what Papa says to you! I heard him say two nights ago: 'You look like a magnolia, darling.' "

"It is what I like him to think," her mother had said with a smile. "Perhaps one day, my dearest, your husband because he loves you very much will say the same to you."

After this conversation Fedora had looked in the mirror to see if she did indeed look like the magnolias which blossomed in the overgrown garden in the spring.

Then she had forgotten about it until now, as she watched Lady Sheelah.

Finally, having finished powdering her face, she licked the end of one of her long fingers and removed any surplus powder that might have adhered to her blackened lashes.

Then, adjusting the emeralds round her neck, she moved from the mirror with a satisfied sigh.

Because Fedora thought it was rude not to speak, she waited until Lady Sheelah had seated herself elegantly on a satin sofa and spread out the full folds of her emerald skirt before she asked:

"Do you and your husband often stay in this wonderful Castle?"

To her surprise, Lady Sheelah stared at her in a hostile manner before she replied:

"It is not your place to ask impertinent questions, and unless you have the hide of a rhinoceros, you should realise that you were expected to eat your meals alone and not force yourselves on your betters!"

Her attack was so unexpected that Fedora gave an audible little gasp and could think of nothing she could say in reply.

"What is more," Lady Sheelah went on, "if I were in your place, I would not wish to appear looking like something out of the Ark!"

The way she spoke was not only surprising but seemed, since she was being so spiteful and disagreeable, to make her look ugly instead of beautiful as Fedora had thought her to be at first.

Various retorts she might make in reply seemed to flash through her mind. But because she was sure her mother would have behaved with dignity in the face of what was an act of excessive vulgarity on the part of Lady Sheelah, she rose to her feet.

Walking tensely but deliberately to one of the paintings hanging on the wall, she stood looking at it.

Because her heart was thumping and her lips felt dry, she could for the moment see nothing but a blurred image of colour and naked bodies.

Then, because she was determined not to allow herself to be brow-beaten by the woman who she was sure was staring at her back, she forced herself to realise that the painting was by Fragonard and it was *The Bathers*, one of his masterpieces which she had always wanted to see.

She concentrated on the exquisite colours of the bare flesh, the rapture on the laughing faces of those bathing, and the professional quality of the brush-work.

She did not speak and there was silence in the room until the door opened and the gentlemen appeared.

Fedora saw that her father was not amongst them, and as she watched the door, waiting for him to appear, the Earl came to her side.

"Your father, Miss Colwyn," he said, "is a little tired after the journey and thought it wise to retire to bed, but I hope you will stay and talk with us."

"No . . . I must . . . go to . . . Papa," Fedora said quickly. "Thank you, My Lord, for a most delightful dinner!"

She hurried to the door, but the Earl walked beside her and when they reached it he said:

"I am sure your father will be well looked after by his valet. You are quite certain you wish to leave us?"

Involuntarily Fedora glanced to where Lady Sheelah was talking to the other men in the party.

"Quite . . . certain!"

"I understand," the Earl replied, "and tomorrow morning we will have the quiet talk you asked for."

"Yes . . . please," Fedora begged. "It is very . . . important!"

The Earl smiled. She curtseyed and hurried across the Hall and up the stairs.

As she reached her father's bedroom she found, as she had expected, that he was on the point of collapse.

He was sitting in a chair while Jim was undressing him, and without saying anything Fedora helped.

Only when they had assisted Alexander Colwyn into bed and he leant back against the soft pillows did he say:

"I will be . . . all right . . . in the . . . morning."

"Yes, of course you will, Papa," Fedora answered.

At the same time, she thought he was very pale. She knew that he had been keyed up with excitement and brandy, but despite the food and medicine he had taken in the last few days he was still weak from the long months of privation.

A few minutes later her father was asleep and she followed Jim from the room.

Outside in the passage, he said:

"Now don't yer go worrying yerself, Miss Fedora. The Master's overtaxed 'imself for the moment, but 'e'll pick up again in a comfortable place like this."

"I hope you are right, Jim."

"Course I am!" Jim said stoutly. "But if 'e follows my advice, the Master'll stay in bed tomorrow."

Fedora looked worried.

"Will they not think it very strange?"

"Wot's it matter what they thinks?" Jim retorted. "They wants to pick 'is brains, don't they? Well, they'll have to wait 'til 'e's ready, and there's no arguing about that!"

Fedora could not help smiling, because Jim's attitude was always one of aggression if it was anything that concerned her father's health.

"We shall just have to wait to see how Papa feels," she said.

" 'Ave you seen the Studio they've fixed up for 'im?" Jim enquired.

"No," Fedora replied. "Where is it?"

Jim walked a little way down the passage and opened a door.

It was obviously the room in which she and her father had been expected to dine, since the candles in the sconces were lit and there was also an oil-lamp on one of the tables.

It was a very strange room because it was almost circular, and Fedora realised at once that it must be in a tower, perhaps the original Norman tower which had given the building its name.

What was stranger still was that while there were two long narrow windows which might have been enlarged arrow-slits, on the North wall there was a large window, in fact surprisingly large for the room.

She stared at it in surprise, and Jim said with a grin:

"One of th' servants tells me this room, which they calls 'The Studio,' was made for the old Earl's aunt, who rather fancied 'erself with a brush, and after 'er quite a number of portrait painters 'as used it when they was a paintin' members of th' family."

"How interesting!" Fedora exclaimed. "I must get some-one tomorrow to tell me who the artists were. I know it would interest Papa."

"They'll tell you right enough," Jim said. "They talks about the pictures in the 'ouse as if they'd all dropped down from 'eaven. Yer'd think no-one else in the world had ever owned a picture."

Fedora gave a laugh of sheer amusement.

She knew that Jim, like her father, had been asserting himself with the other servants and was determined not to be "put on."

"Well, we will just have to wait and see what Papa has to say about the Heversham collection," she said, "and if we find it is not as good as it is supposed to be, we shall certainly be able to laugh."

Then she added quickly:

"But of course, only to ourselves!"

"Yer're right, Miss Fedora," Jim agreed. "We mustn't bite the 'and as feeds us, must we?"

Fedora laughed again. Then she looked round the Studio and said:

"I am tired too and am going to bed. What shall we do about these lights?"

"Leave 'em!" Jim said firmly. " 'Tisn't our business to blow 'em out. We're guests, Miss Fedora, and don't yer forget we're the ones to be waited on."

"It will certainly be a new experience," Fedora replied. "Good-night, Jim, and thank you for everything."

She left him and went to her own bedroom, where to her surprise there was a housemaid waiting to help her out of her gown.

It was only when she was finally alone that she realised that her room was as old as the Studio in the tower.

The walls were enormously thick, judging by the size of the windows they were a later addition, and the ceiling was supported by heavy beams, and although she was not sure, she thought perhaps they were ship's timbers.

But the room was exceedingly comfortable, with a thick carpet, velvet curtains, and a big bed draped with frilled muslin.

Suddenly, in a way that Fedora could not explain to herself, the part of the house they were in, perhaps because it was old, made her shiver.

She did not know why, but the atmosphere was very different from that of the rooms downstairs.

'I am being imaginative,' she thought as she got into bed.

Then, because the excitement and tension of the last few days and the worry over her father had taken its toll, even though she was not aware of it, she instantly fell asleep.

* * *

She thought, seeing the light coming through the sides of the curtains, that she had slept dreamlessly and without moving the whole night.

It was like coming back from a far distance through thick clouds and gradually being aware of her surroundings and what had happened.

Then with an irresistible lilt in her heart she remembered that for the moment they had no money worries.

If she was clever and could prevent her father from realising what was happening, when they left Heversham

Castle there would be no reason for them to sell one of their paintings, for they could live on what her father had earned.

"He must never know," she told herself, and hoped that she could persuade the Earl not to mention it to him.

It would be very embarrassing to ask him to give the money to her. At the same time, whatever he thought or did not think was of no consequence beside the necessity of earning enough to keep her father alive.

Without ringing the bell for the maid, simply because it did not occur to her to do so, Fedora got out of bed to pull back the curtains.

Then she drew in her breath.

Last night when they arrived she had been too worried at their being late to notice anything but the house itself.

Now she was looking over a different part of the garden laid out elaborately in the French fashion. Beyond there were woods and at the side of them an exquisite view of green fields stretching towards a blue horizon.

'It is so beautiful!' Fedora thought, and wondered what her father would think of it.

She was standing by the window when there was a discreet knock on the door and a housemaid came in carrying a tray on which there was not only a pot of China tea but also two slices of bread and butter so thinly sliced that Fedora thought they were almost transparent.

The maid was young with rosy cheeks and was quite obviously a country girl.

As she put down the tray and pulled back the curtain from another window she said:

"As it's a warm day, Miss, I thinks you'd not be wantin' a fire. But I'll light it for you, if you feels cold."

"No, thank you, I am very warm," Fedora replied.

Then she added curiously:

"Does everybody have a fire in their bedroom in the mornings?"

"Oh, yes, Miss. It's the first thing I does as soon as I calls anyone."

Remembering how cold she had been in the Manor when she rose, to Fedora this seemed the height of luxury.

"It's ever so cold in this part of the house," the maid went on, "and we often have fires here when they're not needed elsewhere."

"It must be very old," Fedora said.

"Very old, Miss, and spooky, if you knows what I mean!"

"Do you mean there are ghosts?" Fedora enquired with a smile.

"Yes, Miss, real ones, as well as . . ."

She suddenly stopped, and Fedora knew by the expression on her face that she had been about to say something indiscreet.

Then, as if she was horrified by her own indiscretion, she turned abruptly towards the wardrobe, saying as she did so:

"If you tells me what you'd like to wear, Miss, I'll see if it wants pressin'."

"I was interested in what you were saying about ghosts and what else there was here that made it 'spooky,'" Fedora replied.

The maid glanced towards the door as if she thought somebody might be listening.

"I'll get into trouble if Mrs. Kingdom, that's the Housekeeper, Miss, hears me talkin' in such a way. I hopes you won't tell on me."

"No, of course not," Fedora assured her, "but I have often thought there are ghosts in my home, which is also very old. But if there are, they are friendly and not in the least frightening."

"Well, I hopes you're not disturbed here," the maid said quickly. "Now, Miss, what would you like to wear?"

Fedora knew she would get no further information, and although the maid came back several times while she was dressing, she would still not be drawn out on the subject of ghosts.

'I wonder what sort of ghost it is supposed to be,' Fedora thought.

She imagined it would be a Knight in clanking armour, or perhaps a Royalist who had hidden in the Castle when he was pursued by the Roundheads.

As soon as she was dressed Fedora went to her father's room to find him, as she had half-expected, looking very pale and tired, and having his breakfast in bed.

"I am growing old and senile," he said to Fedora as she appeared. "Once I was man enough to ride all day and to stay up all night. Now a short journey, and I am knocked out!"

"It was a long journey, Papa," Fedora said gently, "and you have not been well lately. But I have never known you in better form than you were last night at dinner."

Her father tried to laugh but it was a weak sound. Nevertheless, his eyes were twinkling.

"I think I showed them that a Colwyn of Mountsorrel can hold his own when challenged."

"You did indeed, Papa, and I was very proud of you!"

"To think," her father went on as he buttered a piece of toast, "that the Earl of Heversham, who is an intelligent sort of chap, has never heard of my paintings."

"They were saying downstairs, Sir," Jim interposed, "that the present Earl, who inherited only last year, 'adn't been in England for some years, an' what's more, havin' quarrelled with 'is father, most things in the Castle are new to 'im."

"Well, that accounts for it," Alexander Colwyn said, "so I see we shall have to educate him."

"I am sure you can do that, Papa," Fedora said with a smile.

She saw with pleasure that her father was eating a large breakfast, which she hoped would take away some of the strain that showed in his pale face and the lines under his eyes.

"I had better go and find my own breakfast," she said, "but, Papa, you will not be getting up today, will you?"

"I am thinking about it," her father replied in a non-committal voice.

As she looked at him anxiously, Jim shook his head and she felt sure he would see that her father behaved sensibly.

Feeling a little shy at being on her own, she walked slowly down the Grand Staircase.

"Breakfast is in the Morning-Room, Miss," the Butler told her respectfully as she met him in the Hall.

He led the way to a room which, looking South, was filled with sunshine.

There were only two men present, seated at an oval table in the window, and they rose as she appeared.

"Good-morning, Miss Colwyn!" one of them said. "I see you are an early riser, which is unusual in this house!"

Fedora sat down in the chair that a servant pulled out from another table and asked anxiously:

"Are you saying I am not . . . supposed to come down to . . . breakfast?"

"No, no, of course not!" the gentleman replied.

She remembered that he had been seated next to her last night at dinner, and she had heard him addressed as "Sir Ian," although she had no idea what his other name was.

As she helped herself from a dish of eggs cooked with creamed mushrooms, he went on:

"In my home my mother would be horrified if people stayed in bed, unless they were ill, but Sheelah has never been known to appear before midday. Is that not true, Rodney?"

He addressed the other man at the table, who laughed before he said:

"It takes her half the morning to put all that stuff on her face. I cannot imagine why Kimball does not tell her she overdoes it when in the country."

"I doubt if even Kimball is brave enough for that!" Sir Ian replied, and they both laughed.

Fedora thought it was a somewhat strange way of speaking about another guest, and it struck her that they were also being slightly disloyal to their host.

Then she told herself that after the rude way in which she had behaved last night, there was no need for her to champion Lady Sheelah.

She was in fact extremely glad that she would not have to endure her rudeness at breakfast, whatever might happen at any other meal.

It suddenly occurred to her that perhaps the reason why Lady Sheelah had been so angry last night was that she had referred to her husband.

Yet surely it would be impossible for her to be a guest in the Castle unless she was accompanied by a relative as a Chaperone?

Although they were too poor to entertain and the Manor was in an isolated part of the country with few neighbours, her mother had taken a great deal of trouble in explaining the social conventions to Fedora.

"I hope that one day, if we can afford it," she had said, "you will be able to attend Balls and parties as I did when I was eighteen. So it is very important, dearest, that you should know what is correct social behaviour."

When Fedora became eighteen two months ago, her mother was dead. But she had told herself she would never forget all she had been taught, and if she were fortunate enough to be asked to a Ball or a house-party, as her mother would have wanted for her, she would try not to disgrace herself.

One thing her mother had made very clear was that a lady must always be chaperoned, and it would be unthinkable, even if she was married, to stay without her husband when a party consisted only of men.

'I cannot understand it,' Fedora thought.

"You are looking very serious," Sir Ian remarked.

Fedora smiled.

"When I looked at the view a little while ago from my window, I wanted to laugh and sing and dance because it was so lovely!"

"You should be doing all those things at your age."

"Of course," the gentleman who was called Rodney

agreed, "and it is a pity our host cannot give a dance here. What could be a better setting?"

"It is like a Fairy-Palace," Fedora said.

She spoke with such a note of awe in her voice that both gentlemen laughed.

Then Sir Ian said:

"And of course if it were not for such very unfortunate circumstances, Kimball would be Prince Charming."

As he spoke, the door opened and a voice said:

"Who is flattering me so outrageously?"

The Earl came into the room and Fedora saw that he was wearing riding-breeches and highly polished boots.

She would have risen to her feet to curtsey, but he said quickly:

"Do not move, any of you," and walked to the table to sit down in a chair next to Fedora.

"I thought you were coming riding with me this morning, Ian," he remarked as the servants hurried to offer him a choice of several dishes, while the Butler poured out a cup of coffee and put the pot in front of him.

"To tell you the truth, Kimball," Sir Ian replied, "your wines were too good last night."

"Well, Basil joined me," the Earl said, "but his leg, which he injured last year at Polo, is playing him up, and he is going to rest for an hour or so before he joins us."

"It is a damned nuisance to have an injury like that!" Rodney remarked.

Fedora looked at him in surprise.

Her father never swore and she had always believed it was something a gentleman never did in front of a lady.

As if the Earl unexpectedly knew what she was thinking, he said:

"I must apologise, Miss Colwyn, for Lord Ludlow's language! The only excuse can be that he was badly brought up!"

Lord Ludlow for a moment looked angry, then he said:

"You are right, Kimball. I apologise, Miss Colwyn. I forgot how young you are, and I shall certainly be more circumspect in the future."

Fedora felt embarrassed.

"Oh . . . please," she said, "I do not . . . wish to be a . . . nuisance."

The Earl had, although no doubt he had meant it kindly, drawn attention to her, and she knew as she spoke that she was blushing.

"What do you intend to do this morning?" Sir Ian asked, as if he wished to change the subject.

"It is a question I should be asking my guests," the Earl replied. "But let me put it another way—what do you want to do, Ian?"

"If I have the choice, I would like to read the newspapers in the sunshine."

"Well, that is easy."

The Earl turned to his other guest.

"And you, Rodney?"

"I have some important letters which must catch the post. Then, if you will allow me, I will ride, as I should have done this morning if my head had not felt as if it had been sledge-hammered!"

"I could have warned you that the vintage port you were drinking can be dynamite on top of the other wines," Sir Ian teased.

"I am beginning to think that the sooner I lock up the wine-cellar, the better!" the Earl remarked.

"If you do that, I shall suddenly remember a pressing engagement in London," Lord Ludlow remarked.

The way he spoke made both the Earl and Sir Ian laugh, and Fedora could not help thinking it seemed stupid that intelligent men should drink so much at night that they felt ill the next morning.

"Then that leaves me with the last person to ask what she wishes to do," the Earl said to Fedora, "and I think I know the answer."

"Papa is a little tired this morning," Fedora replied, "but if Your Lordship would allow me to look round at some of your paintings, I think I should be able to tell him which he should consider first."

"I would like to show you the ones that most interest me, and which I want to bring to your father's attention," the Earl said.

She had been afraid that he was going to say that they were the ones which her father should restore, and for a moment she had looked up at him anxiously.

Then, as if he understood, he talked of something else.

When they all rose to leave the breakfast-table, the Earl said to Fedora:

"Will you come with me, Miss Colwyn? There is something I want to show you in the Library."

The other two men moved off in a different direction, and Fedora followed the Earl along yet another long corridor until they reached the Library.

It was a large room with every wall covered with books from floor to ceiling, with the exception that over the mantelpiece was a Van Dyck. The moment she saw it Fedora gave a little exclamation of delight and tipped back her head in order to look up at it.

It was obviously of an ancestor of the Earl, and the composition was very much the same as in the portrait the artist had painted of her own ancestor.

He was standing with the Castle in the background, but it was very different from how it looked now. The head of his horse appeared in the painting, and there were two dogs looking up at him adoringly.

He was painted with a delicacy and splendour which the artist—as Alexander Colwyn had often explained to his daughter—intoxicated by his own skill combined with his high spirits, managed to transmit onto the canvass.

"It is lovely! Absolutely lovely!" Fedora said, as she felt the Earl was waiting for her to speak. "But I know Papa will tell you that it needs revarnishing and the dogs particularly need cleaning."

"I knew you would say that," the Earl answered. "And now that we are alone, you told me you had something important to say to me."

61

"Y-yes . . . of course."

She suddenly felt shy and embarrassed at what she had to say.

Then she told herself that her father's well-being depended on it and she must not fail him.

She drew in her breath and said in a very small voice:

"I know, My Lord, that you . . . asked my father to come . . . here because you . . . wanted him to . . . restore your paintings."

"That is true."

"And you . . . intend to pay him for . . . doing so."

"Naturally!"

For a moment Fedora felt she could not go on.

Then as if she realised that the Earl was looking at her in a puzzled fashion she continued:

"When the letter came, Papa was not well and I opened it. But when I told him of the invitation . . . I did not show him the letter."

"Why not?"

"Because," Fedora said, "Papa has never in his life been paid for any of the restoration work he has done for his friends, or even to oblige acquaintances!"

The Earl looked puzzled.

"I do not understand what you are saying," he said. "I was told that your father is the finest restorer of paintings in the country, and my secretary informed me that he had agreed to come here and that he would restore to their former glory my paintings, which, as I expect you are aware, I have recently inherited."

Fedora gave a little sigh.

"I am afraid I am . . . explaining things very . . . badly," she said, "but because we are so very . . . very . . . poor at the moment, we need the money . . . desperately. So I should be very grateful if you would . . . pay Papa for anything he does while he is here . . . but please give the money to . . . me . . . and never let him be . . . aware that he is . . . anything but your . . . guest."

For a moment there was silence. Then the Earl said:

"I think I am beginning to understand. What you are

saying, Miss Colwyn, is that while your father really needs the money, he is too proud to accept it."

"Yes, that is the truth," Fedora agreed, "and if he thought that he was to be paid, I am afraid he would not only refuse to accept anything from you ... but would leave ... immediately!"

"Shall we sit down and talk about this?" the Earl suggested.

He must have been aware, Fedora thought uncomfortably, that she was trembling with the intensity of her feelings and had linked her fingers together in an effort at self-control.

She was worried too that it seemed disloyal to appear to intrigue against her father, and yet there was nothing else she could do.

She sat down on one of the leather-covered armchairs which stood in front of the mantelpiece, and as she did so she glanced up at the Van Dyck. The mere fact that this painting was so like their own gave her a feeling of safety.

"What I do not understand," the Earl said after a moment, "is that you spoke last night of the Van Dyck your father owns, and he was saying in an almost aggressive manner that he thought his collection was as good as mine, if not better. How can you reconcile that with the fact that you need the money?"

Fedora thought he was being rather stupid, and she said:

"I imagine, My Lord, that most of the paintings in the Castle are entailed."

"As yours are!" the Earl finished. "Of course! I never thought of anything so simple."

As he spoke, Fedora realised that he had not expected a professional painting-restorer to be of such importance that anything he owned had been entailed to him and to the generations that came after him.

Because she felt it was insulting that he thought such a thing, she lifted her chin and for a moment felt some of her nervousness swept away by the same pride that had animated her father last night.

"The Colwyns have lived at Mountsorrel, My Lord, since the reign of Queen Elizabeth. The house is not quite as large as yours, but we have a collection of paintings which you will find mentioned in every reference book on the subject."

Fedora said this slowly, and as she finished her eyes met the Earl's defiantly.

Then she saw a twinkle in his, and he smiled.

"I suppose I should start by apologising for having misunderstood the whole situation from the word 'go,' " he said, "and perhaps to justify myself I could blame my secretary."

Fedora did not reply and after a moment he said:

"Please forgive me, and now tell me exactly what you want me to do."

"If you . . . really want Papa's . . . help," Fedora said in a low voice, "will you just ask his . . . advice? Then if he . . . offers to . . . restore your paintings, accept it . . . gratefully, as if he is doing it for . . . nothing, which he will . . . think he . . . is."

She paused and felt she could not go on.

"I will do that, and I will pay anything that is owed, which I think will be a great deal, to you," the Earl agreed.

Fedora gave a sigh that seemed to come from the depths of her being.

"Thank you," she said. "I hate to behave like this, and Papa would be extremely angry if he knew, but at the moment there is nothing else I can do."

"Are you really so poor?" the Earl enquired.

She saw him glance at the shabby, old-fashioned gown she was wearing.

"If I answer that question," she replied, "you will pity me and then I in my turn shall want to leave because it would be humiliating."

"I can see that your pride, Miss Colwyn, is a very difficult thing to deal with."

"I agree with Your Lordship," Fedora replied, "but

unfortunately, pride is like self-respect—one cannot eat it!"

The Earl laughed.

"Now you are being human. You really frightened me."

Fedora looked at him and felt shy at the expression in his grey eyes.

"Thank you for being so . . . understanding," she said, "and I promise you that you were indeed correctly informed that Papa is the greatest expert in the restoration of paintings in the whole of England. Perhaps one day you will be able to see, because he looks after them so carefully, how beautiful . . . our own paintings are."

"I hope you will invite me to visit you."

As he spoke, Fedora had a sudden vision of the shabbiness of the Manor compared to the Castle and the frugal meals which consisted of only one course because they could not afford anything more.

She had spoken without thinking, and now she almost laughed aloud at the idea of the Earl visiting them and what he would think of the way they lived.

Because it was something she did not wish to discuss any further, she rose to her feet.

"I am sure, My Lord," she said, "you have a great many things to occupy you. So may I just wander round alone and report to Papa what I have seen? I promise I will not be a bother to anybody."

"You could not be that," the Earl said, "but first I have something to show you."

He did not say what it was, but they went from the Library up a side-staircase which led to the First Floor of a different part of the house.

They walked for some way towards what she thought must be the East Wing, and when they reached it there were two large and beautifully painted doors that shut it off from the rest of the house.

The Earl opened one of the doors and she found herself in a small hall hung with paintings, and out of it opened several other doors.

He opened the first and Fedora walked into what she was sure, without having it explained to her, was the Earl's private Sitting-Room.

It was obviously a man's room with several paintings of horses by Stubbs.

Over the mantelpiece in the place of honour was a Van Dyck.

One glance at it told her why the Earl had brought her here, for she saw that it was in fact an exact replica of the one which hung in her bedroom, and in which the Madonna resembled both her mother and herself.

She stood staring at it, knowing that the Earl was waiting for her to speak and trying for the moment to think of nothing but the painting.

Was it possible? Could it be possible that this was a copy and theirs was the original, or vice-versa?

Because she knew it was important, she tried to see any discrepancies in the technique or, what was so characteristic in Van Dyck's work, the psychological insight.

But it was impossible to find any fault with Mary's robe, the tender respect in Joseph's expression, or the contentment on the face of the Holy Child.

She must have stood in silence for a long time, until at last the Earl asked:

"Well? What is your verdict?"

"It is . . . identical with the one we . . . possess!"

"From the way you speak, I think there is something very personal to you about it."

He was more perceptive than she had expected, and after a moment she said a little reluctantly:

"My father always . . . thought that my . . . mother resembled the . . . Madonna."

"As you do!"

She looked at him in surprise.

"You really think that?"

"Of course I do!" the Earl replied. "I knew it the moment you came into the room last night, and even more so when you had removed your bonnet and came down to dinner."

Fedora looked back again at the painting.

"I have been thinking," she said in a low voice, "that because I have looked at it so often and loved it because it was like Mama, I have grown like it rather than that I was intended to look like it when I was born."

"I think, however hard you tried," the Earl said, "it would be impossible for you to change the oval of your forehead, the straightness of your nose, and the mystery in your eyes."

Although he spoke softly, Fedora felt as if his voice vibrated in a strange way within her, and she felt herself blushing.

Then she said quickly, because she was shy:

"You will . . . understand that it would . . . upset Papa to see this, and perhaps therefore it would be . . . best to keep it from . . . him."

"Do you imagine I could go through the rest of my life wondering whether it is a real Van Dyck or not?" the Earl enquired. "If this painting means something to you, it also means something to me."

Fedora waited, but he did not elaborate and after a moment he said:

"In fact, before your father leaves the Castle I must insist on knowing the truth!"

He spoke imperiously, as if he defied her to refuse him, and after a moment she said:

"I am sure there are . . . many other . . . paintings for him to . . . restore."

"Yes, of course, but this is the most important," the Earl agreed. "Now, suppose you examine a Stubbs which my father, being a keen sportsman, valued above all the others."

There were dozens of very fine examples of the best-known painters, which were in comparatively good condition compared to the Poussin which hung in the Earl's Suite and which was in such a bad state of repair that Fedora suggested it should be taken immediately to the Studio which had been assigned to her father.

"Papa is very fond of Poussin's work," she said, "and I

am sure when he sees this he will want to start restoring it immediately."

The Earl smiled.

"In other words, you are tempting him, which is what I should be doing to you."

"I want to stay here in the Castle," Fedora confessed. "I am still afraid that it may vanish in front of my eyes, or Papa will suddenly feel homesick and take me away before I have seen all your treasures."

"Before he shall do that, I will pile every painting in the place into what you call 'The Studio'!" the Earl said.

Then as if he understood that she was really worried, he said quietly:

"Leave everything to me. I will make sure your father helps me and in doing so makes you happy."

"Thank you . . . thank you!" Fedora cried impulsively. "You are very kind and . . . understanding . . . and I am very . . . grateful!"

Her eyes met the Earl's as she spoke, and somehow it was difficult to look away.

They spent what was an entrancing two hours looking at the Earl's paintings, then he suggested they should go out into the sunshine.

"You have admired Stubbs's horses," he said. "Now come and admire mine."

"I am longing to see them," Fedora said eagerly.

"And to ride them?"

"More than I can possibly say, but I am afraid if I do you will be ashamed of me."

"Why?"

"Because although I brought my habit with me in case I had a chance of riding . . . it is very old and . . . shabby."

"I do not think the horses will mind in the slightest," the Earl replied, "and if you are afraid of what anybody else might think, you and I might ride alone."

"Could we do that?"

She thought he paused for a moment. Then he said:

"As you realised this morning, I usually ride before breakfast."

"And I can do that?"

"My guests are free to do anything that pleases them."

"Then can I ride with you tomorrow morning?"

"If you can be ready by seven-thirty."

"I shall be up long before that, in case I am late."

He laughed, then he said:

"Then I shall certainly be on time, and I shall look forward to it."

"It will be very . . . marvellous for me," Fedora said, "and I only hope . . ."

She realised that what she had been about to say would have been indiscreet, but she was in fact hoping that Lady Sheelah would not hear of it and be annoyed.

She would certainly think it extremely presumptuous that the daughter of the man who had come to clean the paintings should be riding alone with the Earl.

Then she told herself that she must not let Lady Sheelah's rudeness and bad behaviour spoil her chance of riding what she knew would be superlative horses and of enjoying herself at the Castle.

"After all, what is happening to me now will happen only once in my life, and it will be something to remember in the years ahead," she told herself.

"I am not afraid of Lady Sheelah," she added, then knew that was not true.

Chapter Four

Fedora stood in the Studio looking at the painting of Apollo and Daphne and realised that there was an enormous amount of work to be done to it.

It was one of Poussin's great compositions, and she knew her father would say it was a fine example of the intellectual content of the artist's work.

But it had obviously been neglected for many years, and she knew it would require days, perhaps weeks, to bring it back to the perfection it deserved.

When she had come upstairs after luncheon she had peeped into her father's bedroom to see that he was still fast asleep.

It was then that she had decided not to return to the others but to sit in the Studio and read.

But when she saw the painting she knew that the work they had come to the Castle to do was waiting, and she might as well begin.

Luncheon had been an uncomfortable meal because Lady Sheelah was obviously resenting her presence and showed it by either ignoring her completely or, when she spoke, looking at her in a hostile manner.

Fedora sensed that she did not dare to be as rude in front of the Earl as she had been last night, but she managed skilfully, which obviously came from long practice, to keep the attention on herself.

Sparkling like the diamonds she wore in her ears and at her throat, she was in many ways, Fedora thought, so fascinating that she could understand that every man present was enraptured by her.

There was, however, no doubt as to whom Lady Sheelah wished to captivate, and that was the Earl.

It was not only what she said and the expression in her eyes when she looked at him, but the way she continually touched him with her long, thin fingers.

She also seemed in some special way to be closer to him than was conventional or, Fedora thought critically, proper.

She was spectacularly dressed, or rather over-dressed, in a different shade of green from the one she had worn last night, but which still matched her eyes and drew attention to the red in her hair.

From the moment they sat down at the table, Lady Sheelah was determined that nobody else should talk except herself, and, feeling nervous of her, Fedora knew it would be unwise to say anything.

Once or twice she thought the Earl glanced in her direction, but she was careful to keep her eyes downcast except for when she was admiring the paintings on the wall and the architectural magnificence of the Dining-Room itself.

When the meal was over and Lady Sheelah led the way back to the Drawing-Room, Fedora escaped, merely saying as she passed the Earl:

"I must go to Papa."

"I have sent the Poussin to the Studio," he said.

She smiled and was about to say that it would be exciting to look at it closely, when she thought Lady Sheelah might overhear.

Instead, she hurried up the stairs and felt somehow that she was escaping from something which menaced her.

'If I start to clean off the old varnish,' she thought now, 'I can save Papa a lot of work later.'

As if anticipating what she would want to do, Jim had already spread out on a long table what her father called the "tools of his trade."

There were the palette knives, the brushes, the paints, the cleansers, the varnishes, and all the other things that he used and which he had collected over the years because, as he had often said:

"Paintings are like patients. They all need different individual treatment to bring them back to health."

Lying on a chair were the painter's smocks which both Fedora and her father wore when they were working.

The few clothes they had were too precious to be smeared with paint or marked with varnish.

Fedora's, which was very old, had once been a rather vivid shade of blue, but it had faded to the mellow tint of that colour which appeared in so many paintings by great artists.

It made her skin look dazzlingly white, and although she was unaware of it there were blue shadows in her dark hair as she stood in the light of the North window.

The Studio was provided with several easels, and someone had put the Poussin, which had been taken from its frame, on an easel which held it at exactly the right height.

Fedora picked up what she wanted from the table and started to work.

As usual when she was concentrating on the task that she always found fascinating, she forgot everything else until suddenly she became aware that she was being watched.

She thought it must be her imagination, and looked towards the door to see that it was firmly closed.

Then she told herself she was being imaginative.

But while she went on carefully removing the old dark varnish from the painting, she was still acutely aware that, in some way which she could not explain, she was not alone.

The maid, who she knew by now was called Emily, had said the Studio was "spooky," and although it seemed ridiculous, she knew that that was what she was feeling at the moment.

Because the impression was so vivid and undeniable,

73

Fedora stopped what she was doing and looked round for an explanation.

The circular walls were, she was sure, on the outside of the tower, and that only left a wall which joined the room to the rest of the house, and half of another in which there was the door which led into the passage.

The door was not only closed but fitted well, and she turned again to the mantelpiece and realised as if for the first time that while it was marble and obviously old, it was framed on either side with what appeared to be Jacobean panelling.

It was in a linen-fold design which was quite a complicated one, and it flashed through Fedora's mind that it would be quite possible for the carving to conceal a peep-hole.

In a way which she could not explain, she felt afraid, but she walked resolutely towards the fireplace. There was no sound and no movement of which she was aware, yet she knew that the watcher, whoever it might be, had gone.

She stood staring at the panelling, but she could see nothing to tell her that her conviction was right and there was an opening in it through which somebody could look.

Nevertheless, she was sure she was not mistaken.

She thought she would ask Emily who was in the room next door. Her bedroom and her father's extended in a different direction and it was hard to understand exactly how the Castle was constructed in this wing.

When she thought about it, she imagined that the Studio was at the end of a passage, and because she was curious, she opened the door and found that what she had thought was a wall did in fact contain door.

'Perhaps it opens into a room,' she thought, and wondered if it would be wrong of her if she turned the handle to find out.

Then she told herself that she was behaving in a manner which her mother would think was extremely reprehensible and returned to the Studio.

She went on working on the painting, but now nobody was watching her, and an hour later, when she rested, she told herself that she had just been day-dreaming.

There could be no possible reason why anybody should be curious as to what she was doing.

"Why should there be, when there is no secret about it?" she asked.

When Jim came to say that her father was awake, she ran to his bedroom to tell him what she was doing in the Studio.

"It is a very fine Poussin, Papa," she said, "and the moment I saw it I knew you would be horrified at the condition to which it has been reduced. I therefore asked the Earl if he would send it to the Studio so that we could look at it in the North light. I hope you are not angry that I have started to work on it."

She looked at her father a little apprehensively as she spoke, afraid it might annoy him, but he merely said:

"I hope the Earl appreciates your industry on his behalf, but I have no intention of working on any of his paintings until I have seen them all and have decided which ones are worth saving."

Fedora smiled.

"You are being very autocratic, Papa!"

"I intend to be," her father answered. "I do not forget so quickly the way they intended to treat us last night, if I had not asserted myself."

"I think you must really blame His Lordship's secretary for that," Fedora said. "He obviously misunderstood his Master's instructions."

As she spoke, she knew that her father was not appeased.

He was still feeling insulted that the Earl had not heard of the Mountsorrel collection and had thought he was only a craftsman rather than a gentleman standing on equal terms with his friends.

Because Fedora was afraid that her father's pride would make things uncomfortable, she put her hand on his to say:

"Once anybody sees you, Papa, they know that whatever your name may be, you are a very distinguished and very charming gentleman!"

"Thank you, my dear," Alexander Colwyn said with a slightly dry note in his voice. "And as I feel so much better, I intend to come downstairs for dinner tonight."

"Are you really well enough, Papa?"

"My tiredness has gone!" her father said positively. "In fact, I am ready for anything—even that delectable siren with the red hair!"

"You are not trying to flirt with her, Papa?" Fedora teased.

"A woman like that would flirt with anybody!" her father replied.

"Do you know anything about her?"

The question came to Fedora's lips with difficulty, because she found herself disliking Lady Sheelah more and more.

"She told me she is a widow and the daughter of the Earl of Frome," Alexander Colwyn replied. "Unless my memory is at fault, he went bankrupt some years ago and everything he possessed was sold. I remember Lewenstein handled some of his paintings."

Fedora was well aware that it was the paintings which had registered the Earl's name in his mind, and she wondered why, if Lady Sheelah's father was bankrupt, she had such magnificent jewellery.

Then she told herself that of course her late husband, of whom she had no wish to speak, must have been a very rich man.

She thought it would please her father if she had tea with him in his bedroom instead of going downstairs to join the others.

She also knew that she had no wish to be near Lady Sheelah or to watch the way she behaved with the Earl.

She was quite certain that her mother would consider her behaviour very fast and certainly out-of-date.

In the new reign, Queen Victoria had brought in a standard of propriety which had been sadly lacking in her Uncle George's time.

In the seven years that William IV and Queen Adelaide had reigned, they had tried to raise the standard at Court from the depths of depravity to which it had sunk and which, judging by the cartoons, had been a permanent scandal.

But King William had died before much had been achieved, and it was his niece Victoria who, on succeeding to the throne at age eighteen, had changed everything as if she had waved a magic wand over the country.

At least, that was what Fedora had believed, and her mother and father had said over and over again what a joy it was to have a young Queen who listened to the advice of her Statesmen.

"Why was George IV so wicked, Mama?" Fedora had asked when her mother had been describing the era in which she had been a débutante.

Mrs. Colwyn had hesitated.

"He was not exactly wicked, Fedora," she replied, "but he behaved in an immoral manner himself, and of course all the Bucks and Beaux followed him, which meant he set a very bad example to his Subjects."

"But what did they actually do, Mama?" Fedora had insisted.

Her mother had evaded the question, but because her father was more explicit and many of the newspapers were more outspoken, she had learnt that Mrs. Fitzherbert, Lady Jersey, Lady Hertford, and the Marchioness of Conyingham had all been mistresses of the King.

If that was not shocking enough, William IV had ten illegitimate children by the actress Mrs. Jordan before he married his young and very prim and proper German wife.

It was when she went back from her father's bedroom to the Studio to stand looking at the partly naked figure of Apollo with his arms round Daphne, who to escape him was turned into a bay tree, that with a sense of shock Fedora was suddenly aware of Lady Sheelah's position in the house.

"How could I have been so stupid as to ask her about

her husband?" she chided herself. "Of course, there is no doubt that she is the mistress of the Earl!"

Then, as her reason told her that this must be the truth, since there could be no other explanation of her being here unchaperoned, some yearning that she could not understand made her long to refute it.

And yet, the more she thought of it, the more it appeared completely plausible.

Why otherwise was there no other woman staying in the house? Why else was Lady Sheelah so possessive, so flirtatious, so embarrassingly intimate with the Earl?

And what was more, Fedora thought, the fact that he was a very rich man would certainly explain the jewellery that had seemed so dazzling.

The whole explanation confronted her and shocked her, but it was something which she did not wish to believe.

She suddenly had no desire to go on working, feeling that it was Daphne and Apollo who had conjured up such an idea in the first place.

Without even removing her blue smock, she went from the Studio along the passage, not certain where she was going, but wishing only to escape from herself and her own thoughts.

Then, before she reached the main staircase which would take her down to the Hall, she saw another minor one, just as there was on the other side of the house, up which the Earl had taken her to his private Suite.

She went down it, wondering where it would lead her, and found with a sense of relief that at the bottom of the staircase there was a door inset with panels of glass which led out into the garden.

It was only a question of pulling back two bolts and turning a key before she stepped out into tl.e part of the garden she had seen from her bedroom window.

It was laid out as if it belonged to a French *Château* with small flower-beds edged with tiny box-hedges.

There was a fountain playing in the centre, and in its

stone bowl were goldfish moving round under the leaves of a water-lily which seemed to be a rare species, being pink instead of white.

It was so lovely that Fedora stood looking down at the fish and the lilies and the fountain, which caught the rays of the sun to fall iridescent as a rainbow into the bowl.

It was all part of the fairy-tale in which the Castle and its owner were set, she thought. And somehow it was inevitable, because she was thinking of him, that the Earl should appear.

There was just the sound of his footsteps, and she knew without turning round who was joining her.

He came to her side to look down into the water as she was doing. After a moment he said:

"I had a feeling you would find your way here sooner or later. This was my favourite place when I was a boy, and if the fish are not the ones I put here on my seventh birthday, they are certainly their sons and grandsons."

"The . . . lilies are very . . . beautiful!"

"My mother planted those," the Earl said, "and I promised myself that one day I would have them painted."

He paused before he added:

"I now know whose hand should hold them, and who should be wearing the blue robe you are wearing now."

Fedora had forgotten that she had on the smock she had been working in, and she smiled as she replied:

"This is my working-gown, and since I am wearing it I think you can guess what I have been doing."

"I am very grateful to you," the Earl said. "But what will your father say about it?"

"He has not seen the painting yet," Fedora replied, "but because he is feeling better he is coming down to dinner."

She hesitated, then she said:

"You will be very . . . careful not to . . . show that you . . . expect to restore the paintings? I know he intends to . . . offer to do so."

"I hoped you would trust me."

"I do," Fedora said quickly. "At the same time, Papa . . ."

She hesitated, then the Earl smiled and completed the sentence:

". . . is very proud!"

Because she could not help it Fedora laughed.

"Very, very proud, and he is still a little upset by what happened when we first . . . arrived."

"Do I need to apologise to you for being so obtuse and so foolish over the whole thing?" the Earl asked.

"No, I understand," Fedora replied, "but, please . . . help me with Papa. I know if he stays here even for a . . . little while he will get better in health and be more like his . . . old self."

"You know I will help you in any way I can."

There was a depth in the Earl's voice which was very different from the way he had spoken before, and Fedora looked up at him.

Then her eyes were held by his.

For a moment they just stood looking at each other before the Earl said in a deeply moved voice:

"I have been looking for you all my life. The painting which now hangs in my Sitting-Room is one of the first things I remember seeing when I was perhaps two or three years old, hanging in my mother's bedroom."

Fedora gave a little exclamation of surprise, and exclaimed:

"The one we own was in my . . . mother's room . . . until when she died I took it into . . . mine!"

For a long moment there was silence. Then the Earl asked:

"How can you be so absurdly like the Madonna? Is it possible that one of your ancestors, a Colwyn, modelled for the painting?"

Fedora gave a little laugh.

"In which case you will have to admit that ours is the real, authentic Van Dyck!"

"For the moment I can only think that you are real," the Earl said.

There was that note in his voice which made her feel as if her heart turned over in her breast and which also made her inexpressibly shy.

She looked down at the goldfish and after a moment the Earl said:

"You are very beautiful, Fedora, but it is much more than that. There is something which makes me feel you belong to me in the same way that the paintings are mine and yet are not just possessions but a part of my living and breathing."

For a moment Fedora felt as if the sunshine dazzled her eyes and glittered like the water of the fountain.

Then almost as if a dark cloud covered the sky she remembered Lady Sheelah.

She stiffened and without consciously realising it she lifted her chin proudly.

As if he knew without words exactly what she was feeling, the Earl said:

"Forgive me! I have no right to speak to you like that."

Without another word he turned and left her.

Although she did not look back, she heard his footsteps walking away until she could hear them no more, and she felt bewildered and dismayed in a manner which she could not understand.

How could he have said such things to her?

How could he have made her feel as if she were listening to the song of angels, and then suddenly the wonder and beauty of it was gone and he had left her?

She wanted to run after him and ask him for an explanation. She wanted to look into his grey eyes and know that they held hers.

Then almost as if a streak of lightning stabbed her she told herself that perhaps he was engaged to Lady Sheelah and intended to marry her.

That would explain everything: the fact that she was staying alone in the Castle and the manner in which she was behaving towards his guests whom she had not invited herself.

"How can he? How can he wish to marry anybody who is so rude, so horrible?" Fedora asked herself.

She felt suddenly very young and ignorant, lost in a world that was like a bewildering maze.

Most of all, she found herself beset by conflicting emotions from which, again like a maze, there seemed to be no escape.

Because the garden had somehow lost its enchantment, Fedora walked back into the house, bolted the door as it had been before, and went up the stairs.

She peeped into her father's room, saw he was still sleeping, and went into the Studio.

The painting was waiting for her, but she felt too bemused and upset by what had happened to work.

Instead, she pulled off her blue robe, trying not to remember that the Earl had said he would like her to be painted in it, and crossed the room to where there was a bookcase.

She saw that the books all had something to do with art. Some were descriptions of paintings that were in Museums abroad, while others were of the lives of famous artists.

Opening one at random, she found that on the inside of the cover was the signature: "*Charlotte Hever*," and she was sure that this had been the Earl's aunt who had liked painting.

She thought she would read one of the books and sat down in a chair by the window.

Yet, when she turned the leaves it was impossible to concentrate, and instead of seeing the print she saw the Earl's face, his grey eyes, and heard him say in a voice that made her quiver:

"You belong to me in the same way that the paintings are mine and yet are not just possessions but a part of my living and breathing!"

How dare he say that he owned her! Fedora tried to say.

But she knew that some secret voice inside her told her that he spoke the truth.

She had known from the first moment she saw him that there was an expression in his eyes that made her shy, feeling that he looked deep within her for something that only she could give him.

She knew now that it was because she resembled the Madonna that hung on the wall in his Sitting-Room.

She had never seen a painting of him, and yet, in a way she could not describe, she recognised him, perhaps across time and space.

"How can I think such ridiculous things?" she asked herself, and added: "But they are not ridiculous . . . they are . . . true!"

Then as she tried to force them from her mind, the door of the Studio opened very, very slowly—so slowly that as Fedora turned her head to watch, she thought perhaps it was some supernatural movement, part of the spooky atmosphere she had felt unmistakably when she was working on the painting.

As she watched, not really frightened but spellbound, somebody came in through the door.

It was a woman, small, slight, and wearing what Fedora thought was a white dress, until she saw to her astonishment that it was a nightgown, trimmed with lace and with long sleeves.

The woman's feet were bare, and her hair, fair and straggly and not very long, was falling over her shoulders.

Fedora was so surprised that she could not move. But the woman saw her and came towards her.

Her bare feet made no sound, and for a moment Fedora was certain that she was not real but was the ghost she had been expecting.

As the woman drew nearer, Fedora could see that her face was very thin and lined, and while she must once have been pretty, there was something strange and rather horrifying about her eyes, which were very pale blue and seemed to stare vacantly at her.

She came nearer still, and Fedora, who had been sitting without moving, was too bewildered to get to her feet.

"Why—are you—here?" the woman asked. "What are you—doing with that—painting?"

The words were enunciated very slowly and almost as a child would who was learning to read, and while they sounded quite coherent there was something unnatural about them.

"I . . . I am staying here in the . . . Castle," Fedora managed to say.

"You—must go—away! You must—go away at—once!"

The woman's voice had changed and now there was an accusing note in it.

Then as she stared at Fedora she suddenly gave a scream.

"You are trying to take him from me! That is what you are trying to do! Go away! Go away!"

She screamed out the words.

Fedora, now thoroughly frightened, was trying to struggle out of the chair to her feet when two people came hurrying into the room.

They went one to each side of the woman in the night-gown and held on to her arms. Fedora saw from the way they were dressed that they were Nurses.

"Now come along, My Lady," one of them said. "You should be asleep and resting."

"She is trying to take him from me! She will keep him from seeing me! Send her away! Send her—away!"

The woman's voice rose to a shriek.

The Nurses turned her round and, half-pulling, half-carrying, they moved quickly across the room and out through the open door.

Fedora could hear the woman in white still screaming until finally there was the sound of a heavy door being slammed, and then there was silence.

She was so astounded that she felt as if the breath had been knocked out of her body and she could only lie back on the chair, feeling it was difficult to take in what had happened, let alone explain it.

Who was the woman in the nightgown? There was no doubt that she was not completely sane.

Fedora realised that at first sight her eyes had seemed somewhat vácant, then there had been a madness in what she had said and in her screams as the Nurses took her away.

Because it had been so unexpected and upsetting, she felt her heart pounding in her breast and her hands were trembling.

It would certainly explain her sense of being watched through a peephole in the panelling. It also told her what lay beyond the door at the end of the passage.

Yet there were questions to which she knew she was afraid to learn the answers.

Whatever the answer might reveal, it would undoubtedly be something she did not wish to hear, which would destroy her delight in visiting the Castle.

She had a sudden longing to run away from the Castle, to go home, and to be free from all the conflicting emotions she had felt ever since she arrived.

For one moment everything seemed to whirl bewilderingly round her: the Earl, her father, Lady Sheelah, the goldfish and the sunshine in the garden, and the woman in the white nightgown.

"I do not understand!"

She felt she had become involved in a train of events from which she could not escape and which was carrying her swiftly and frighteningly to an unknown destination.

She could not go back but only forward, but to where and with what suffering to herself she could not bear to contemplate.

* * *

It was with the greatest reluctance, because Fedora knew that her father was going downstairs to dinner, that she faced the fact that she must do the same.

She had sat in the Studio until the sun began to set, and she knew that her father would be wondering why she had not been to see him and that it would soon be time for her to have a bath and change her gown.

Not until Emily brought her only evening-gown from

the wardrobe did she think despairingly that what she was feeling was accentuated by the fact that she had nothing else to wear.

Although she told herself she had no wish to see the Earl again, she could not ignore an irresistible feminine desire to look as beautiful as he had said she was.

"How can I do that in a gown that is out-of-date and threadbare and makes me look beside Lady Sheelah like the traditional goose-girl in a fairy-story?" Fedora asked herself.

Yet she knew that however much she might protest, something within her was aching to see the Earl, to look at him, to hear his voice.

There were so many unanswered questions turning over and over in her mind.

She shrank from thinking of him with Lady Sheelah as either his mistress or his fiancée, and, even more alarming—what was his connection with the woman in the nightgown?

"I cannot bear it! I want to go home! I never want to see the Castle again!" Fedora wanted to cry aloud, but she knew it was untrue.

If she really had the opportunity, she would not leave now, because, for good or bad, even if it involved misery and despair, she had to know the end of the story.

"You really need another gown, Miss," Emily was saying.

"I know," Fedora replied, "but the fact is, Emily, my father and I have not been able to afford anything as frivolous as clothes for a very long time."

"That's a shame," Emily said. "If you had one of the gowns like Her Ladyship wears, you'd look a real picture!"

Fedora did not speak and she went on:

"Hundreds and hundreds of them, she's got! Every wardrobe in her room and the room next to hers is filled to overflowing, and still she's buying more!"

Emily gave a little snigger.

"It's a good thing there's someone as can afford to pay for them!"

Fedora wanted to tell her to be silent, but the words would not come to her lips.

Because it was all so upsetting, she found herself praying to her mother.

"Help me, Mama, help me," she said beneath her breath. "I do not understand what is happening and I am afraid of my own feelings. Tell me what to do and what is right!"

She almost felt as if her mother might answer her, but instead there was silence until Emily came back into the room, which she had left to fetch the piece of velvet ribbon that Fedora had worn round her neck last night.

"I've pressed this, Miss," she was saying. "It's a pity you haven't got a nice piece of jewellery like a locket or a cameo to pin on it."

Fedora wanted to reply that if she had such things they had been sold long ago to buy food to eat, but instead she managed to answer:

"It looked very nice last night the way you tied it, Emily, so please do the same again."

However, she was well aware when she looked in the mirror that her lace bertha was limp from old age, and however skilfully she had darned it, it was obvious that it had been repaired.

The straight lines of the skirt certainly made her look, as Lady Sheelah had said so scathingly, as if she had "stepped out of the Ark."

She wished that she could pretend she was ill and stay upstairs instead of going down with her father and know that the Earl was watching her with his gray eyes.

It crossed her mind that she should tell her father that it would be wise for them both to leave.

Then she knew that she could not do anything to injure him, and whatever anybody thought about her, including the Earl, her first loyalty and her love belonged to him.

It was the pride that ran in the Colwyn blood that made her smile as she entered her father's room and tell him how handsome and smart he looked.

It was pride that made her walk down the stairs with her head high, pretending she was dressed in cloth of gold instead of rags.

It was pride that made her meet the Earl's eyes defiantly instead of looking away shyly as he approached them.

"I am so delighted that you could join us," he said to her father, and there was no doubt that he was speaking sincerely.

It was with a sigh of relief that Fedora saw that Lady Sheelah was not in the room.

Lord Ludlow and Sir Ian told her they had missed her during the afternoon but presumed she found the Earl's paintings more interesting than they were.

"I have seen very few of them as yet," Fedora replied, and Sir Ian groaned in an exaggerated way.

"Paintings! Always paintings!" he exclaimed. "Personally, if I am given the choice, I prefer my women living and breathing. Paintings are all right in their place on the walls, but I can assure you there are a lot more entrancing things you and I might do together."

Fedora thought he was trying to flirt with her and hoped she would not seem too gauche in her reply.

She was saved from making one as the door opened to admit Lady Sheelah, who was undoubtedly making a grand entrance.

If Fedora had imagined herself wearing a gown of gold, Lady Sheelah had compromised with one of silver, which made her as dazzling as a star in the sky.

Her very full skirt was embroidered all over with silver flowers which had diamanté centres, the gown caught the light from the candles in the chandeliers, and with diamonds round her neck and in her red hair she seemed as she walked towards them as if she were enveloped in moonlight.

It was so theatrical and yet at the same time so lovely that Fedora thought despairingly that she must have dreamt what the Earl had said to her by the fountain.

It would be impossible for him to think of any woman except Lady Sheelah.

That was what she obviously expected as she walked up to him and, lifting her face to his, kissed his cheek.

Then in a low voice, which however was quite audible to Fedora, she said:

"Thank you, darling Kimball. I hope you feel it was worth the expense."

If he answered, Fedora did not hear it. The other men, including Major Basil Gower, who had followed Lady Sheelah into the room, were paying her compliments and Sir Ian was telling her with a slightly sarcastic note in his voice that she looked like the Queen of Sheba.

"I am quite prepared to represent the Queen or Cleopatra, as long as Kimball is Solomon or Anthony!" Lady Sheelah replied, and they all laughed.

Then, as if he felt she was being left out, the Earl deliberately detached himself from the others to say to Fedora:

"May I offer you another glass of champagne, Miss Colwyn?"

She tried to answer him calmly and sensibly, but despite her resolution there was an undoubted little tremor in her voice as she replied:

"N-no . . . thank you."

The Earl looked down at her where she was sitting on the edge of the sofa, and for a moment he had his back to his other guests.

He seemed to hesitate, then as if he was aware without words of what she was feeling, he said:

"I asked you to trust me."

It was not what she had expected him to say. She looked up at him questioningly and found there was an expression in his eyes that she had not thought to see.

She could not understand, yet she knew she was not mistaken. It was one of sadness and despair.

Chapter Five

"I knew you would ride superbly," the Earl said as they drew their horses in from a gallop to a trot.

"How could you know that?" Fedora asked.

With the blood flushing her cheeks and the wind cool on her forehead, she felt as if she had stepped into an enchanted dream from which she prayed she would not wake.

When she had run downstairs quickly in case she should be late to meet the Earl, Fedora had thought she was making a mistake in letting him see how badly dressed she was for riding with anybody, let alone him.

When she was small and they were not so poor, her father and mother had both hunted with the local pack of hounds.

Not only were they very smart in their riding-clothes, but everybody else in the field had looked to Fedora different from the way they did on other occasions.

The men with their high starched stocks, white breeches, and highly polished boots, and the women with their tightly fitting habits and hats encircled with a gauze veil, might have just stepped out of a fashion-plate.

Her mother had always taken a great deal of trouble over her appearance, but as Fedora had taken her riding-skirt from the wardrobe she knew the right place for it was the waste-paper basket.

It was patched and faded and, as she was well aware,

like her other gowns it was far too straight and narrow to look anything but ridiculous now.

Riding-skirts were now very full, and Queen Victoria obviously wore a number of starched petticoats under hers to make them as alluring as any Ball-gown.

"There is nothing I can do except stay in bed," Fedora told herself.

Then she knew that she could not resist the opportunity of riding the Earl's horses, and without looking in the mirror she put on her riding-skirt.

She hesitated when she looked at the jacket. It was out of shape, beginning to split at the seams, and the cuffs were definitely ragged.

She threw it down on a chair and decided that however strange she might appear, she would ride without it, for the rising sun promised another hot day.

Her blouse was at least clean, and it was then that she remembered that while she had packed her riding-habit, more because she had emptied her wardrobe of everything she possessed than because she expected to have a chance of riding, she had not brought a riding-hat.

Even if she had done so she would have been ashamed to put it on, and once again she wondered if she had not better send a message to the Earl to say she did not feel inclined to ride.

Then she remembered Lady Sheelah's appearance last night in her silver gown and knew that even if she were wearing the habit any London tailor could provide, the Earl was not likely to notice her.

She therefore pinned her hair tightly to her head so that it would not look untidy and went to the stables with a defiant look in her eyes.

When she saw the Earl's horses she forgot everything but them.

She had expected them to be fine but not as magnificent as they were, and the old groom who was in charge was pleased at her enthusiasm and took her from stall to stall, telling her the history of the breeding of each horse and when the Earl had acquired them.

They had almost reached the end of one stable when the Earl came into the yard.

He was looking so smart that she stared at him wide-eyed until he said:

"I expected you would be here rather than waiting for the horses to be brought to the front door."

"Is that what I . . . should have . . . done?" she asked quickly.

"No," he replied. "I always choose the horse I am going to ride, although I suspect Nick has already chosen it for me!"

He looked at the old groom as he spoke, who said:

"Well, mebbe Oi do, M'Lord, and would ye fancy ridin' Jupiter this mornin'? 'E bain't been out much this past week."

"Then Jupiter it must be," the Earl said agreeably. "And which horse would be suitable for Miss Colwyn?"

"As the young lady understands, 'orses, M'Lord, Oi don't think as Vulcan'd be too much for 'er."

The Earl agreed, and when a very fine chestnut was brought into the courtyard he lifted her into the saddle.

She was so light that he said when he had done so:

"I fear you may float away if there is even the suspicion of a breeze. Are you quite sure you can handle him?"

"I hope . . . so."

She had felt herself quiver as the Earl lifted her in the air with his hands round her waist.

It was the first time that she had not mounted a horse by herself, or been assisted at home by the boy who had looked after her father's horses until they could no longer afford his wages.

She hoped because the Earl was lifting her that she would behave correctly, but she had not expected to feel an extraordinary excitement because he was touching her, or to be aware that her heart was suddenly thumping in her breast.

Because she was afraid he might guess her feelings, as he mounted his own horse she forged ahead of him, and

93

when they reached the Park without speaking they both urged their mounts to a gallop.

She had never ridden such a well-bred horse as Vulcan, and she thought he must indeed have come from Olympus and she was riding over the clouds.

Only when the Earl complimented her did she feel the colour come into her cheeks, but she told herself he was only being polite and tried to answer him lightly.

"It will delight Papa that you are pleased with the way I ride," she said. "He is very insistent that women should look as elegant riding a horse as they do seated in a carriage, but I am afraid I am out of practice when it comes to either."

The Earl did not speak for a moment. Then in a low voice he said:

"I would like to wrap you in sables, deck you in jewels, and never again would you have to do anything but look beautiful."

The way he spoke made Fedora feel inexpressibly shy. Then she told herself it would be a mistake to take what he was saying seriously.

"If... wishes were... horses, My Lord," she said at length, "beggars would... ride... and as a beggar I am very... content at the... moment and would ask for nothing more than to ride Vulcan for all... eternity."

"And I would ask for nothing more," the Earl answered, "than to ride with you."

Now there was no mistaking that there was a note of pain in his voice, and because it was impossible to ignore it Fedora turned her face to look at him.

She saw that the sadness and despair she had seen in his eyes last night were still there.

Then, because she felt it was something she could not mention and indeed did not know what to say, she merely pressed Vulcan forward, and once again they were both galloping over the grass.

Finally they came to the edge of a wood and Fedora was obliged to rein in Vulcan and the Earl came up close beside her.

This time he did not speak but merely rode ahead, going into the wood by a ride cut through the trees.

Fedora followed him until after a little while they came to a clearing in which there were a few tree-trunks stacked neatly to one side of it, although it was apparent that the wood-cutters had not been there for some time.

The Earl dismounted and, putting his hand on Vulcan's bridle, said:

"I want to talk to you. At least here we will not be disturbed."

She felt a little quiver go through her at the seriousness in his voice. Then because there was nothing else she could do she slipped from the saddle onto the ground.

The Earl knotted the horses' reins on their necks and left them free, and putting out his hand to Fedora he drew her toward a fallen trunk at the side of the cleaning.

She knew he meant her to sit down, and she did so, thinking how lovely and mysterious the wood looked on each side of them with the sunlight flickering through the branches of the trees to make a pattern of spotted gold.

It was very quiet except for the song of the birds, and she felt once again as if she had stepped into fairy-land, but a very different one from the ornate grandeur of the Castle.

She was conscious that while she was staring round her the Earl was looking at her.

He had taken off his tall hat and put it on the ground beside him, and she thought without even glancing in his direction how handsome he was and how different from any man she had ever seen before.

Because he was so close, she felt both shy and excited, and slightly afraid, yet at the same time she was glad with a joy that was seeping over her like the sunshine itself.

For a moment she forgot Lady Sheelah, forgot the strange woman in the white nightgown who had frightened her yesterday evening.

She remembered only that the Earl and she were alone,

and that when he spoke to her in his deep voice it made her vibrate towards him in a way which made her feel that she was no longer herself but a part of him.

She could not explain it, and it was impossible to put it into words or even to think clearly.

She only knew it was what she felt, and it came from her heart and was quite inexpressible.

The Earl did not speak. Then almost as if he hypnotised her into doing so she found her eyes turned to his and knew she could no longer look away.

Fearfully, because the very silence between them was overwhelming, her eyes looked into his.

Then at last, as if he could no longer control himself, the Earl spoke.

"I love you!" he said. "I have loved you from the first moment I saw you, and that was not when you came into the Drawing-Room, but when I looked at your portrait on the wall in my mother's bedroom and knew you were beauty itself."

As he spoke, it seemed to Fedora as if the sunshine came through the trees to illuminate them both, and it was impossible to see anything because of the light which radiated from the Earl.

"I love you!" he said again. "And I had to tell you so before I sent you away."

It took a second for what he said to percolate through the rapture his words had aroused in her body.

"S-send me . . . away?" she repeated in a voice that did not sound like her own.

"My precious, my sweet, pure, untouched love," the Earl said in a voice that broke, "why should this have happened? You do not understand! Oh, God, why should this have happened to me?"

The agony in his voice was so poignant and so disturbing that impulsively Fedora put out her hands.

"What are you . . . saying?" she asked. "What is . . . wrong? You must . . . tell me!"

He took her hands in both of his and his fingers tightened until their grip was painful.

Then he said:

"If I have committed any sins I am certainly being punished for them. I am prepared to accept my fate, but not that you should suffer with me. That is something I cannot bear!"

"What . . . is . . . wrong?" Fedora asked again.

The Earl took his eyes from hers and looked down at her hands.

In his agony he had squeezed the blood from her fingers, and now as if in retribution he raised her hand to his lips, kissing first the back of it, then turning it, over and kissing the palm tenderly and lingeringly.

The touch of his mouth gave Fedora not only a feeling of excitement but something deeper, something so fundamental that she felt as if she had always been aware of it and yet had never known it before.

Then as if he felt he dare not touch her, the Earl put her hand down in her lap and released the other.

In the same strangled voice in which he had spoken before he said:

"What do you know about me, my darling?"

"Very . . . little," Fedora replied in a low voice, "except that you are the . . . man who has . . . always been in my . . . dreams."

She spoke shyly and so softly that she felt the Earl would not hear the words.

Then as she saw the sudden light in the sadness of his eyes she knew that not only had he heard, but for the moment he looked young and happy and the lines seemed to disappear from his face.

"What else do I mean to you?" he asked in a low voice. "What do you feel for me?"

Once again they were looking into each other's eyes, and because it was impossible to tell him anything but the truth, Fedora answered:

"I . . . love you! But I did not . . . know that love would be . . . like this."

He felt her eyes held the sunshine and they were

neither of them human but part of the sky, the woods, and the beauty of the enchanted world round them.

"I love you!" he said. "And it is true, we belong to each other as we have done since the painting of you was painted so that I should see it and know you were mine almost before I was aware of anything else in my small world."

"Can . . . such things . . . happen?"

"I am sure of it," the Earl answered, "but, my darling, fate has brought us together only to separate us again."

"Why? Why?"

Then as she asked the question she found herself thinking of Lady Sheelah, and she looked away from the Earl, feeling as if the sun had gone in and the sky was no longer blue but grey.

As if he knew what she was thinking, he said sharply:

"No, she is not important. What you do not know is that I am—married!"

To Fedora the word fell between them like the death-knell of hope, and even as her mind assimilated what he had said, she was aware that it was what she had expected.

It was what she had guessed must be the explanation for the woman who had come into the Studio to scream at her yesterday evening.

The Earl drew a deep breath. Then he said:

"When I lay awake last night, thinking of you, wanting you until I felt I must go insane, I knew that I could not bear you to learn the truth from anybody but me."

It was what she might have known he would feel, Fedora thought.

At the same time, she felt as if she had received a blow, and it was hard to think of anything but one word which kept repeating itself in her mind:

"Married! Married! He is . . . married!"

The Earl turned a little away from her to stare across the clearing with unseeing eyes before he said:

"I was married when I was twenty-two to someone whom my parents considered eminently suitable and whom they pressed upon me until it was impossible for me to do anything but agree to what they wished."

Fedora forced herself to listen to what he was saying.

She knew that because he was so handsome and so wealthy, obviously there would be many women who would want to marry him, and his parents would wish to make sure that his bride was suitable from every point of view.

"Maureen," the Earl went on, "was the daughter of the Marquis of Fane, whose father's Estates marched with those belonging to the Castle."

He drew in his breath before he continued:

"The Marquis was determined on an alliance, as he had no son, and he brought every pressure to bear on his daughter to ensure that she accepted my offer of marriage."

"She did not . . . wish to . . . do so?" Fedora asked in a whisper.

"She was compelled to agree," the Earl continued, "although she was in fact in love with her Riding-Master, which is, I believe, a passing phase with a great number of young girls."

He spoke with bitterness in his voice, and Fedora said quickly:

"She . . . would not have been . . . allowed to . . . marry him?"

"No, of course not! Not when there was a chance of her marrying the heir to Heversham Castle!"

"What . . . happened?"

"We were married, with all the pomp and circumstance, hysterical good wishes, bridesmaids, and all the other traditional paraphernalia that women enjoy and men find embarrassing."

He paused but there was nothing Fedora could say, and after a moment he continued:

"It was on our honeymoon that Maureen, who wept continuously, told me she hated me and reiterated over and over again how much she loved the man she had left behind."

Because Fedora knew that this must have hurt him in his pride if nothing else, she slipped her hand into his.

"I am . . . sorry."

"I suppose I was young and stupid, but it was a situation I did not know how to cope with."

"What . . . did you . . . do?"

"Nothing," he replied. "I tried to confront her and, somewhat ineffectively, to make the best of a bad job. I even suggested that we should at least pretend our marriage was successful."

He sighed.

"I had the idea that despite all Maureen said, we might eventually become fond of each other. She was very beautiful and it was not difficult for me to be attracted to her as a woman."

Fedora felt a pang of jealousy which made her fingers tighten on his.

Then as if she had asked the question the Earl said:

"I was not at all in love, although I knew very little about the emotion then, and I thought that what I feel for you, my darling, was something which only happened in books, or perhaps in paintings."

He looked at Fedora as he spoke, and time stood still.

Then after a moment, when it was difficult to think of anything but the expression in his eyes, she asked:

"What . . . happened?"

"We came back to England from our honeymoon, which was a farce from the very beginning," the Earl replied, "and went to live in a house on the Estate which my father had furnished for us. It was then that I began to realise what I had already feared—that Maureen was unbalanced."

"It must have been . . . terrible for . . . you."

"It was frightening, but it was something I was too proud to admit to."

"What did you do about it?"

"She would make an effort when we were with other people," he replied. "My friends had no idea for a long time that she was in any way different from other women of the same age."

His voice sharpened as he said:

"Although Maureen's father and mother knew she was not normal, they had been so delighted at her marriage to me that, as I learnt later, they forced the Doctors to remain silent, although it should have been their duty to warn me and my parents that she was unfit to marry anybody."

"It was ... cruel ... wicked!" Fedora cried.

"I have used those adjectives a thousand times in the years that passed," the Earl said. "When at length I knew exactly what the position was, I was determined, because I had the same sort of pride as your father, that I would not endure the humiliation of people being sorry for me."

"I can ... understand ... that."

"While I was trying to make up my mind what I should do, Maureen grew worse, and because the Doctors told me she should go into a Home, I decided to take her abroad."

"So that was why you left England!"

"Exactly! At first we went to a Villa in Florence. Then, when her condition became too well known there, we moved on."

He sighed before he said:

"I saw parts of the world I would not have seen otherwise. I met men and women of other nationalities and learnt their points of view."

"But you ... must have ... found it very ... difficult," Fedora murmured.

He understood what she was saying, and answered:

"It was very difficult to keep anything hidden, because naturally the servants always talked. I knew without words that people knew but would not speak of it, and after a time I grew to accept the situation."

His voice was raw as he added:

"But I hated it! I hated every moment of my life! Just as I hate now having to tell you what I have suffered!"

"Please . . . please . . . do not say any more!" Fedora pleaded. "I do understand . . . and I . . . admire you even . . . more than I did . . . before!"

"You had to know, it was your right to know!" the Earl said. "And, my precious, I could not bear there to be any secrets between us."

Fedora gave a deep sigh.

"You know I would do . . . anything you want me to do . . . and it . . . hurts me to . . . see you so . . . unhappy."

"It hurts me to tell you this when all I want to do is to take the moon, the sun, and the stars from the sky and lay them at your feet."

There was so much love in his voice that she felt herself tremble with a wild excitement. As if he was aware of it, his fingers tightened on hers until once again they were painful. Then he went on:

"My father died, and I had to come home. I brought Maureen with me, and I think, because you and I are so closely attuned to each other, you were aware there was something about the Castle which makes it different from other people's houses."

"I . . . I have . . . seen her," Fedora said very softly.

"How could you have?"

The question was sharp.

"I felt certain when I was working in the Studio that there was . . . somebody . . . watching me. Then yesterday evening she came in and told . . . me to go away because I was taking . . . you from . . . her."

It was difficult to say the words, and they were almost inaudible, and as Fedora's voice died away the Earl said:

"Oh, my sweet, that should not have happened! It was very wrong of the Nurses to let her escape them."

"I felt . . . sorry for . . . her."

"You would be," he replied, "but, my darling, it was not I she was accusing you of taking from her, but her lover, the man she has never forgotten all these years, the man who I need not say was unworthy of her love."

"Oh, no!"

The exclamation came from Fedora's heart.

How was it possible that the Earl's wife was still yearning for another man when she could have him?

"I made it my business to find out about him," the Earl said. "Maureen's father had put him in a position of trust in that he managed the Marquis's Racing-Stables, and, as an outstanding rider, he was told to teach Maureen to ride."

His voice was angry as he went on:

"It seems incomprehensible that anyone who had the slightest pretensions of decency and honour would seduce an impressionable young girl in such circumstances, but that is what he did."

"Did her . . . parents know of this before . . . you married her?"

The Earl hesitated before he replied:

"I am not certain. They would not admit it, of course. They realised she was infatuated with him, which was why they were so keen for the marriage to take place as quickly as possible."

"It was a . . . disgraceful way to . . . act."

"I suppose I might have thought it strange that they never allowed me to be alone with Maureen for any length of time, but it is always easy to be wise after the event."

"It was very . . . very . . . wrong."

"A wrong it is impossible to right," the Earl agreed. "But we are married, Fedora, in the words of the Marriage Service: 'until death us do part.'"

There was silence. Then after a moment he said in a strangled voice:

"That is why I have nothing to offer you except my heart, which is already yours."

"And . . . mine belongs to . . . you."

"Do you mean that? Do you really mean it?"

"I love . . . you!" she said. "I loved you before you made any . . . explanations or told me what I . . . suspected. Now I love you as I did not . . . think it possible to . . . love, and

I love a man who is . . . brave and honourable and . . . good!"

The Earl made a restless gesture as if he would contradict what Fedora was saying. Then he said:

"You can still say that to me when you are aware that Sheelah Turvey is my mistress?"

"I do not . . . like her," Fedora said honestly, "but perhaps she has . . . helped you . . . to forget."

"My darling, I knew you would think like that!" the Earl exclaimed. "Only you could have an instinct which would tell you the truth. Yes, she and her kind have helped me forget over the years."

He paused before he said:

"There have been Sheelah Turveys in Rome, Venice, and almost every part of the world I have travelled with my wife, ceaselessly raving and crying for another man."

The agony in his voice made Fedora exclaim:

"You must not speak like that! I cannot bear it! I can understand how wonderful you have been in behaving with a pride that my father would admire, but to hate, to be . . . cynical and bitter . . . would . . . spoil our . . . love."

She only whispered the last words, but the Earl heard them.

"Our love! Yours and mine!"

"Y-yes."

"Oh, my precious little Madonna, if I could only tell you what it means to me to hear you say it and to know that the world in which I live is not as intolerable as it has begun to seem these last few years."

He made an exclamation before he said:

"I knew when you came into the Drawing-Room that something tremendous had happened which had changed everything. I thought for a moment I must be dreaming when I saw your face just as if you had stepped down from my painting and come to me when I needed you most."

"Did you . . . really feel like . . . that?"

"And much more that I cannot put into words," the Earl said. "When I went to bed I stood for a long time in my Sitting-Room, just looking at you over the mantelshelf."

His voice softened as he went on:

"I knew then that while to have found you was a wonder and a rapture which carried my heart and soul to Heaven, I was being crucified since there was nothing I could offer you—nothing."

His voice was low as he finished:

"I am tied irrevocably to a woman who hates me, and who, according to the Doctors, may easily outlive me!"

For a moment Fedora felt there was nothing she could say. Then almost as if the words came from outside of herself she answered quickly:

"We have . . . two things . . . left."

"What are they?"

"Faith and . . . love."

"Faith?" the Earl questioned.

"That one day . . . somehow . . . by the mercy of God, the . . . way will be . . . smooth and we can be . . . together."

"Do you really believe that?"

"It is . . . not what I . . . believe," Fedora corrected, "it is what I *know*. I know it in my heart. I know it in my mind, even against all the logical arguments. I know it because . . . you're you . . . and I am I . . . and because when you . . . touch me I feel that we are . . . one person."

The Earl drew in his breath. Then he said:

"Because of what you have said and because you are perfect, I want to kneel at your feet. Instead, my darling, I will believe as you believe, that one day we shall be together and there will be no more suffering."

When he had finished speaking he bent and kissed her hands, first one, then the other. Then he rose to his feet and pulled her to hers.

For a moment they stood looking at each other.

Then without seeming to move Fedora was in his arms and he was kissing her.

It was inevitable, and at the same time so perfect, so ecstatic, so clearly what had been meant for them since the world began.

As Fedora felt the Earl's mouth on hers she knew that she had been right in saying they were one person and spiritually nothing could divide them.

His kiss was at first very gentle and there was something reverent about it, as if to him she were sacred and so exactly his ideal that she was not human but Divine.

Then as he found her lips very soft, innocent, and sweet, he became more possessive, more demanding, at the same time still tender and protective.

He kissed her until Fedora felt as if there were not only birds singing in the trees but the music of the Heavens could be heard above them.

The beauty of everything she had seen since she came to the Castle was all there, and all part of the Earl, his arms and his lips.

She felt as if her love poured from her body into his and her heart was his heart, and whatever happened in the future she would never lose him because they were indivisible.

The world spun round them and there was no time but only eternity in which they had lived and loved and lost each other, found each other, and lived and loved again in the river of life in which there is no death.

Because it was so rapturous, so wonderful, her whole body seemed to come alive and be filled with an inexpressible rapture and joy.

When the Earl finally raised his head, Fedora could only look up at him and feel that he had carried her into Heaven.

"I . . . love . . . you!" she whispered, and her voice broke on the words.

Because she was trembling from the sensations he had aroused in her, she hid her face against him.

"And I love you, my darling!" he answered, "so overwhelmingly, so completely and absolutely, that I shall never again be able to see any face but yours, hear any voice but yours, nor kiss any lips that are not yours."

She knew that it was a vow and that he dedicated himself to her for all time.

Then as she looked up at him to tell him once again that she loved him, he was kissing her demandingly, passionately, as if he knew what he was losing physically and must take her heart and soul and make them his forever.

* * *

A long time later, they rode home in silence.

They both felt as if they had travelled to the end of the world and found Heaven, but that the gates had been closed to them and they had been forced to return to reality.

For the moment it was impossible for them to adjust themselves to normality, and Fedora knew that after what they had felt and had said to each other, they could never be the same.

Though for the moment she had to lose the Earl, and she thought it would be easier to die than to live without him, they were still transfigured by love.

Only when the Castle lay ahead of them and she could see the Earl's standard flying over the centre block of the great house did he say:

"We will do nothing and say nothing for the moment, because we must not upset your father. But you know, my wonderful darling, that I will look after you. We will think of some way that I can help you without your father being aware of it and without hurting his pride."

It flashed through Fedora's mind that she should refuse what the Earl was suggesting. Then she knew that their love was greater than pride.

It might be conventionally wrong for her to take anything from him in the way of the money which she supposed he would offer.

But nothing was of any importance beside their love, and she knew it would be ridiculous for her father to go on suffering as he had before they came to the Castle.

What was more, the Earl would want her to live in the same comfort as he did, and he would be upset and depressed if she refused to let him help them.

'I will leave it to him,' she thought. 'He understands

what Papa feels and he will think of some way of supporting him which Papa will accept without feeling insulted.'

She looked at the Earl and thought that no man could be more kind, more handsome, or more magnificent.

As if he knew her thoughts he turned and smiled at her, and she felt that while the horses divided them, their hearts were beating against each other's and his lips were on hers.

The whole world seemed to be radiant with their love, and even the great Castle looked as if it was shining with a light that she had never seen before.

As they rode towards the stables the Earl said:

"Nobody will know that we have ridden together, and tomorrow we will do the same thing, and every day until you have to leave."

"Papa must see your paintings first," Fedora said quickly, "otherwise he will think it very strange."

"I want you to see them all too," the Earl replied, "and perhaps it is the paintings which will make things easy for us in the future, because I can send them to your father to work on at home, and that would be an excuse to send you a lot of other things as well."

Fedora felt as if he was going too quickly and might send her away almost before she could be aware of it, and she could never see him again.

"Please . . . please," she pleaded, "let me stay a little while longer . . . I cannot bear to . . . think of what it will be . . . like when I can no longer . . . see you or . . . hear you."

"And how do you think I shall feel?" the Earl asked. "When you leave me, my lovely one, there will only be darkness and the damnation of hell!"

He spoke quietly, but it seemed to Fedora as if it were the crash of thunder in the skies above them.

Then, as if his thoughts were more than he could bear, the Earl rode quickly into the yard where the grooms were waiting and dismounted.

* * *
108

Upstairs in her bedroom, Fedora felt that she must have dreamt everything which had happened.

Yet she was vividly conscious that just a little way down the passage, the Countess of Heversham, tended by two Nurses, was mad and was crying for the man who had betrayed her rather than for her own husband.

It was a tragedy like one of the stories in Greek mythology, she thought, and although she had said they must have faith and believe that one day they would be together, some practical part of her brain was asking over and over again:

"How long will it be?"

She took off her riding-skirt to change into another of the threadbare gowns that were all she had to wear.

She had no dress in which the Earl could admire her, but she knew perceptively that he saw her not as an ordinary woman but as the Madonna who hung over the mantelpiece, whom Van Dyck had painted a little more than two hundred years ago.

Perhaps the artist had been inspired unconsciously by a love that had not blossomed until this moment, and yet had its conception in the artistry he conveyed to a bare canvas.

If that was true, if there was a fate which shaped the lives of men and women, how could she doubt that, despite all he had said, one day she and the Earl would find happiness?

She felt herself tingle with the wonder of his lips and the glory of her love, in which she was no longer herself but transformed and uplifted into someone very different.

Still feeling as if she were touching the gates of Heaven, she nevertheless behaved automatically in the way that would be expected of her.

She went to her father's bedroom to kiss him good-morning, and while Jim had insisted that he have breakfast in bed, he informed her he was just about to rise and begin his inspection of the Castle.

"I shall know then whether Heversham's collection

rivals ours at Mountsorrel," he said, "and if it does not, I shall not hesitate to tell him the truth."

"No, of course not, Papa, you always do say what you think."

"Honesty is the best policy," Alexander Colwyn answered.

He was obviously very much better in health than he had been for a long time, and Fedora felt that she no longer need be so anxious about him, whatever might happen to her in the future.

She went to the Breakfast-Room to find that she was the first there, but she was soon joined by the other three men.

The Earl did not appear, and because she was closely attuned to him she knew, almost as if someone had told her so, that for the moment he could not readjust himself as quickly as she had.

He was, she was sure, in his own private Sitting-Room, staring at the Van Dyck over the mantelpiece and thinking of her and loving her.

"What do you plan to do today, Miss Colwyn?" Sir Ian asked as they finished breakfast.

"My father will be down soon," Fedora answered, "as he wishes to see the paintings; so I shall go round the Castle with him."

"It might be a revelation to us all," Lord Ludlow remembered. "It would be a joke if Heversham's collection is not all it is set up to be."

"But it is!" Fedora said. "The paintings are really magnificent! They only need cleaning and restoring, and then you will be able to see them as they looked when they were first painted."

"It is going to take some time," Sir Ian remarked.

"I should have thought years," Major Gower said, "and I have the feeling we shall all grow old and grey in the process."

"My father certainly will not stay as long as that!" Fedora laughed.

"You may be sure of that!" Lord Ludlow said. "Lady

110

Sheelah is already planning how quickly she can be rid of you!"

Fedora had felt before that he resented Lady Sheelah's intrusion into the party, and now she was certain of it.

She herself had thought that she did not much like him, although she had no particular reason for it.

"That is not a very pleasant thing to say," Major Gower remarked.

"But it is true," Lord Ludlow insisted, "and I am sure Miss Colwyn is well aware that Her Ladyship does not suffer other women gladly."

As if she thought the conversation was intolerable and she had no wish to take part in it, Fedora rose from the breakfast-table.

"I will go and see if my father is ready to come downstairs," she said quietly, and moved towards the door.

Her departure was unexpected, and she left the room before any of the men could move from their seats.

Then outside, as she was just closing the door behind her, she heard Sir Ian say:

"For God's sake, Rodney, do not make things worse than they are already. You know what Sheelah is like! She would murder any woman who she thought took Kimball's attention from her."

"That is true enough," Major Gower agreed. "She has found a rich mug, and she will fight like a tiger if he tries to escape."

Fedora realised she was eaves-dropping.

She had not intended to do so, but she had been frozen into immobility by learning what Sir Ian had said in her defence.

Now feeling that what they were saying was degrading and an offence to the love she had for the Earl and he for her, she ran across the Hall and up the stairs.

Only as she reached her father's bedroom did she wonder despairingly how she could bear to think of Lady Sheelah and the Earl, and the bitter note in his voice when he had said there had been many Sheelah Turveys to help him forget.

Chapter Six

Fedora did not go to her father's bedroom but to her own.

She was upset by what she had overheard and thought that the Earl was right and it would be impossible for her to go on staying at the Castle as long as Lady Sheelah was there.

At the same time, to leave him, knowing that he was wanting her as she was wanting him, was an agony she found impossible to contemplate.

"What shall I do?" she asked herself.

There was no answer and she was alone in a fog that appeared thick and impenetrable with no way out.

She went to the window and for the first time she did not see the beauty of the garden, the flowers, or hear the song of the birds.

Instead, she could only hear the pain in the Earl's voice and see the despair in his eyes.

Once again she was praying for help.

She felt that her mother, who had been so happy, would understand as nobody else could what she was feeling for the man whom she had only just met, but who seemed to have been with her since the beginning of time.

Suddenly the door behind her was flung open, and as she turned round apprehensively, Lady Sheelah came into the room.

She was wearing an elaborate lace and satin negligée

over her nightgown and her red hair was streaming over her shoulders.

For the first time Fedora saw her face not rouged and powdered and her eye-lashes not darkened with mascara.

But there was no time for her to think of how Lady Sheelah looked as she advanced with her green eyes blazing and her face contorted with fury.

Then she spoke in a voice that was like the snarl of a wild animal, and Fedora thought Major Gower had been right in describing her as a tiger.

"I hear you have been riding with His Lordship," Lady Sheelah cried furiously. "How dare you sneak out with him behind my back! Let me inform you—you ragged upstart—that the Earl belongs to me, and as soon as he is free of his lunatic wife we will be married!"

What Lady Sheelah had said and the ferocity in her tone were very alarming.

But Fedora managed to stand still, looking at her with an outward composure she was far from feeling, and with contempt.

It seemed impossible that any woman, supposedly well-bred, should be so lacking in self-control.

"You and your father have no right to impose on His Lordship's good nature," Lady Sheelah went on, her voice rising. "You have forced yourself upon him, and he is too much of a gentleman to make you keep your place, which as far as I am concerned is in the Servants' Hall!"

She paused for breath before she added:

"And make no mistake, if you do not leave the Earl alone, you will rue the day that you ever came here!"

She raised her hand and for one moment Fedora was afraid she was going to strike her.

Then, with an exclamation of anger that seemed to vibrate between them, she turned and left the room with the same impetus of fury as that with which she had entered it.

She left behind the strong scent of an exotic Oriental fragrance that lingered on the air.

For a moment it was impossible for Fedora to move.

She could only stand there, knowing that now that Lady Sheelah was gone she was trembling from shock at what she had said, while her rage had been so furious and so intense that Fedora felt it had struck her like a physical blow.

Then she thought of the Earl touching such a virago and put her hands up over her eyes, as if by doing so she could block out the knowledge that whatever mood she was in, Lady Sheelah was still very beautiful.

"I cannot stay here now," Fedora decided.

She wondered what she could say to her father to convince him that they should return home.

For a long time she stood at the window, thinking and suffering until, unable to bear being alone any longer, she went in search of him, feeling like a child who, hurt and unhappy, will run to his parents as the one secure refuge in a disturbing and frightening world.

She found him as she had expected in the Picture-Gallery.

The Curator of the Castle was with him, and her father was standing in front of the paintings, admiring them and at the same time criticising their condition and saying what needed to be done to each one.

The Curator was making notes, and when Fedora joined them he said politely:

"Good-morning, Miss Colwyn! As you see, your father is telling me how remiss we have been in neglecting what is undoubtedly our finest treasure."

"It is disgraceful! Absolutely disgraceful!" Alexander Colwyn exclaimed. "Look, Fedora, at Francesca! Unless it is treated, one of the finest works this genius ever produced will be ruined!"

Fedora knew that her father was upset over this particular painting because not more than a dozen works by Francesca had survived.

She looked closely at the painting and saw that it was of the Queen of Sheba adoring the Holy Lord. Instantly she remembered how Lord Ludlow had said that Lady Sheelah in her silver gown looked like the Queen of Sheba.

Despite the fact that her mind told her it could not always be so, she felt despairingly that for the rest of her life, everything she saw would in some way remind her of the Earl or of something connected with him.

As if Alexander Colwyn had said all that needed to be said about the Francesca, he moved on, and while the Curator was writing down his notes, Fedora was wondering how she could show her father the Van Dyck that she resembled before they left.

She knew she could not bear to leave the Castle with the question of its authenticity unsolved, and if she did so she would never look at its duplicate at Mountsorrel without wondering whether it was genuine or a fake.

"The Earl will feel the same," she told herself, "so he must be ready to accept Papa's verdict, however upsetting it may be."

Then as if her thoughts of the Earl had conjured him up, she saw him at the other end of the Picture-Gallery and was sure that he had found it impossible to keep away from her.

She knew this was true by the expression in his eyes when he came nearer. Then he was greeting her father, who immediately went into a long dissertation on the paintings he had already examined and how much needed to be done to them.

"I cannot understand why my father neglected them for so long," the Earl said at length when Alexander Colwyn paused for breath. "I can only think that as he grew older, because they had always been here he saw them as they had been when he lived at the Castle as a boy, which was well over thirty-five years before he inherited."

"You may be right," Alexander Colwyn conceded. "At the same time, paintings are like children, they need to be cosseted and loved, and that is something which I feel yours have lacked."

"I promise you that certainly they will receive that in the future," the Earl replied.

Fedora knew by the way he spoke that he was thinking that when he looked at the paintings, especially one particular one, he would be thinking of her.

She was sure he would understand when she said:

"I think, My Lord, you should show Papa your Van Dycks, especially the one in your Sitting-Room."

She thought the Earl would smile his agreement, but instead she saw the pain that came into his eyes.

She was certain he knew that her reason for suggesting it so soon after her father's arrival was that he had said that he must send her away and they would soon be leaving.

"Of course I want to see your Van Dycks," Alexander Colwyn said. "But is there something special about one of them which requires my attention?"

Fedora slipped her hand into his.

"Yes, Papa," she said. "His Lordship wants you to make a decision and it is going to be a difficult one."

"Why?" her father enquired, then added: "I will not ask any questions. Just show me the painting, then I will understand."

The Picture-Gallery, being on the First Floor, was not so very far from the Earl's private Suite in the South Wing.

They walked there in silence, and Fedora noticed that the Curator tactfully remained behind.

The Earl opened the painted doors and they passed through the hall from which the Poussin had been removed.

As they entered his private Sitting-Room, Alexander Colwyn saw first the paintings by Stubbs.

Then there was no need to point out to him the Van Dyck over the mantelpiece and he moved towards it.

He stood looking up at the painting which meant so much both to Fedora and to the Earl, and they held their breath.

"Amazing! The Master at his best!" Alexander Colwyn murmured. "I doubt if there has ever been another painter so technically brilliant who could give such spiritual perception to his subject."

He stopped speaking and Fedora looked at him in surprise before she said:

"You must ... know, Papa, what we are ... waiting to ... hear?"

"What is that?" her father enquired absently.

He was inspecting a small corner of the painting where the paint appeared to be cracking.

"I could hardly believe when I first saw this painting that it was the ... duplicate of ... ours," Fedora said. "I cannot believe that ours is not genuine, and if it is, then this must be a ... fake."

She found it hard to say the word because she thought it might upset the Earl, and yet because both he and she were personally involved, she had to know the truth.

"A fake? Who is talking about fakes?" her father asked sharply.

"But ... Papa!"

Her father suddenly laughed.

"So that is what you mean! Good Heavens! I have obviously been very remiss in not teaching you more about one of my favourite artists."

He turned round to look at the Earl.

"And you too, My Lord, are surprisingly ignorant for the owner of such a magnificent collection."

"In what way?" the Earl enquired.

"What you should both know," Alexander Colwyn said sharply, "is that Van Dyck often painted two versions of subjects which particularly interested him."

"Two ... versions, Papa!" Fedora exclaimed.

This was certainly something she had not expected.

"I admit he seldom made them as identical as this and the one I possess," Alexander Colwyn said, "but he painted the *Mocking of Christ* twice—there is one in Berlin and one in Madrid—and two pictures of *St. Sebastian*, besides two portraits of the Marchese Spinola."

He laughed as he saw the surprise in Fedora's and the Earl's eyes.

"It seems extraordinary that neither of you were aware of this, and I could quote half-a-dozen others."

He smiled as he added to the Earl:

"And you, My Lord, might have taken the trouble to see them on your travels."

"I stand abashed," the Earl replied. "At the same time, I am delighted and, I may add, extremely relieved to know that, as your daughter supposed when she first saw it, this is not merely a copy of the one which hangs at Mountsorrel."

"One day we will put them side by side," Alexander Colwyn said, "and I will show you that while there are small differences between the paintings, there are similarities of technique which it would be impossible for anyone else, however skilful, to copy."

Fedora felt a sigh of relief.

Somehow, because their fears were now known to be unfounded, it made her feel that her faith in the future was justified, and that however impossible it seemed at the moment, one day she and the Earl would be together.

Because they were so closely attuned to each other, their eyes met and she felt as if she were in his arms and his lips were on hers.

"I love you!" she wanted to say, but she knew that words were unnecessary.

It was nearly time for luncheon and when they left the Earl's private apartments they walked to the Grand Staircase, Alexander Colwyn stopping continually to inspect the paintings and comment on their condition or on the way in which they were hung.

On the stairs was another Van Dyck, which was not his best work. Alexander Colwyn thought it might have been done when the artist was ill and disappointed at his reception in Antwerp, where he had hoped to succeed to the position left by Rubens.

The rest of the party were already gathered in the Drawing-Room and when they joined them Fedora was acutely aware of the venom in the glance that Lady Sheelah gave her.

"I see you have been making the grand tour," Lord Ludlow said. "Well, Colwyn, what is your verdict?"

"Need you ask?" was the reply. "His Lordship is one of the luckiest men in the country! He possesses a treasure that is beyond price and praise!"

"You must be referring to me!" Lady Sheelah exclaimed.

As she spoke she slipped her arm through the Earl's and, raising her eyes to his, said:

"Tell me it is true, Kimball darling, that I am beyond price or praise."

"I think I must first give our distinguished critic a drink after a hard morning's work," the Earl replied.

He disentangled himself from Lady Sheelah's clinging arms, but as he moved away from her Fedora saw apprehensively the fury in her expression.

What saved what might have been a difficult meal was that Alexander Colwyn had so much to say about the paintings.

Because he was so knowledgeable, he was extremely interesting and often very amusing about the artists who had mostly lived strange, Bohemian lives.

There was no doubt that everyone was interested in what he had to say, with the exception of Lady Sheelah, who was bored and impatient that he was commanding the attention which should have been hers.

Both Sir Ian and Lord Ludlow kept asking intelligent questions, and luncheon was nearly finished before the Earl remarked:

"We have a guest for dinner this evening."

"Who is that?" Lady Sheelah asked sharply.

"I think he is a relation of yours, Basil," the Earl replied. "His name is General Sir Archibald Gower, and he has just been appointed Chief Constable of this County."

"He was my father's first cousin," Major Gower answered, "and he had an extremely distinguished Army career. I shall be delighted to see him again. Is his wife coming with him?"

He obviously asked the question without thinking, and

instantly there was that uncomfortable silence which occurs when somebody has made an unfortunate gaffe.

Then as the Earl replied quietly: "No, he will be coming on his own," everybody began to talk at once.

She had not thought of it before, but now Fedora suddenly realised that there were no callers at the Castle.

Because she and her father lived so quietly, it had not seemed strange.

But she now remembered from what her mother had told her in the past that a nobleman in the Earl's position would be continually receiving personal guests and local officials who required his advice or assistance on County projects.

It would be understood that if his wife was ill, it would definitely curtail the hospitality expected of the owner of Heversham.

But that Lady Sheelah should be staying with him unchaperoned would ensure that none of the ladies in the County would call at the Castle while she was there.

'He should not flaunt her to his own detriment,' Fedora thought.

Then she understood that having exiled himself abroad for so long, he felt defiant against both the social code and the law which tied him to a woman from whom he could never be free except by death.

Fedora had once heard her mother say how sorry she was for men and women whose husbands or wives went mad, and from whom the law provided no release.

She had actually been speaking of a young woman whose husband was injured in a fall while riding and who became nothing more than a vegetable. He remained alive year after year, unable to recognise her, but she was still his wife.

"It is a cruel position," she had said in her soft voice. "Surely something can be done for such unhappy people?"

"A woman can divorce her husband only for infidelity and cruelty," Fedora's father had replied. "That is the law, and you must remember, my dear, in the Marriage

Service you vow to take a man 'for richer, for poorer, in sickness and in health' and you can only be free of him by death."

"I know," Mrs. Colwyn agreed, "but, dearest, the law is there to help us to live a full and proper life, not to punish us for no fault of our own."

"You are very soft-hearted," her husband replied, "and I love you for it. At the same time, my darling, it is no use upsetting yourself. There is nothing you can do for your friend, and we can only hope that the death of her husband will bring a merciful release."

"It does not seem likely at the moment," Mrs. Colwyn had said with a little sob in her voice.

"It is cruel, horribly cruel!" Fedora now wanted to cry, thinking of the Earl, a young man tied for the rest of his life to a woman who must be confined to her own rooms with Nurses who were little more than warders.

Because she could not bear to think of it, Fedora turned to make some banal remark to Lord Ludlow, who was sitting on her left.

As she did so, she realised he was looking at Lady Sheelah with an expression that she would not have understood a week ago.

Now, because her love for the Earl had awakened in her a new perception of human emotions, she knew it was desire.

It was not love as she knew it. Nevertheless, the yearning was there, and the fire in the depths of his eyes that he could not disguise.

She had felt since she came to the Castle that she did not particularly care for Lord Ludlow, who was often satirical in what he said, and when he smiled there was a mocking twist to his lips.

Now she thought she understood. He was envious of his friend the Earl, not only for his possessions but also for Lady Sheelah!

It seemed to make things even more complicated than they were already, and Fedora was glad when luncheon was over.

"It is a nice day and I want to go driving," Lady Sheelah said imperiously to the Earl.

Fedora tried not to feel disappointed as the Earl agreed to take Lady Sheelah driving in his curricle.

She knew it would be a joy and a delight to drive with him, but she must stay at home, while Lady Sheelah could be close to him.

She would be saying flattering things as they drove side by side in the sunshine and doubtless touching him in that intimate way which was an essential part of her method in fascinating a man.

Fedora told herself she was not exactly jealous but miserable because she and the Earl could not be together.

What was more, the time when they could even see each other was passing minute by minute until at the stroke of midnight the Ball would be over and she must leave him and go home.

Her father, however, was determined to see all the paintings, and she went round the Castle with him striving to concentrate on everything he was saying until he grew tired and she persuaded him to go to his bedroom and rest.

"The amount of work to be done in this place appals me!" he said before they parted.

"I know, Papa," Fedora agreed. "At the same time, you cannot do it all yourself. You can only give the Earl your advice and help him to find somebody to live here and restore the paintings one by one."

There was a little pause before Alexander Colwyn said:

"I will do them myself, for at the moment I can think of no-one I could trust with the Van Dyck, and certainly not the Poussin."

Fedora did not argue.

Then, because she knew she would be alone there, she went down to the French garden to look at the goldfish.

She thought about the Earl as a little boy putting them into the stone basin and going eagerly to look at them day after day to make certain they were still alive.

It was then that she realised that the Earl must have a

son of his own to inherit the Castle and carry on the name.

Like her mother, she wanted to cry out at the thought of a young man tied to a mad wife.

There had been no chance of seeing the Earl alone before dinner. Although Fedora knew she must tell him that Lady Sheelah had discovered they had been riding together, she thought it would be easier later in the evening.

She therefore sat in the Studio, working on the painting by Poussin and with her thoughts on the Earl. She was desperately afraid, because of the way Lady Sheelah had behaved, that they would not be able to ride together tomorrow morning.

'I must see him alone, I must!' Fedora thought over and over again.

She decided that if it was impossible for her to say anything to him tonight, she would write a letter and get Emily to give it to his valet.

That might be indiscreet, but she thought she could say it was a list from her father of paintings that needed repairing, or something which would allay the servants' suspicions, although she half-suspected that they might already be aware that things were strained.

Lady Sheelah's maid-servant would certainly know that her mistress was upset, and the Earl's valet might feel the same about his Master.

'There are too many people involved,' Fedora thought.

She recalled how different it was at the Manor where there had been just three of them: her father, Jim, and herself.

Yet she knew that after what she had felt and experienced here at the Castle, her home would never seem the same again.

She might have found love, but she had also lost that sense of security and feeling of belonging which is what home means to every child before he grows up and discovers that the world is very different and sometimes frightening.

"You're looking very serious, Miss," Emily remarked as she was dressing.

"I was wishing I had a new gown to wear," Fedora said quickly.

"That's what I said to you last night," Emily replied. "I was wondering, Miss, if you'd like Mrs. Browning, who's the seamstress here in the Castle, to make you something?"

"It is very kind of you to think of it," Fedora replied, "but it would be impossible for me to buy any material and . . ."

She was about to say that she had no money, then thought that was too difficult to explain. She would never spend on herself any of the money she had borrowed from Mr. Lewenstein.

"The Carrier calls here on Tuesdays," Emily went on. "Sometimes he has ever such pretty stuff, and cheap too."

It flashed through Fedora's mind that she would ask the Earl for what she was sure would only cost a few shillings. Then she was ashamed of herself.

How could she sink to Lady Sheelah's level by accepting money for clothes?

It would be bad enough if he provided her father with food as he had hinted he would do, but clothes were something very different.

She knew her pride would make her walk naked rather than become the type of woman whom he admitted he had found in every part of the world.

What she was feeling emanated from her so forcefully that Emily said in a frightened voice:

"I'm sorry, Miss, if I've angered you by suggesting such a thing. I were only a-trying to be helpful."

"Yes, I know that, Emily," Fedora replied, "and I am very grateful to you."

She went down to dinner thinking she would at least see the Earl, and even if they did not speak they would be acutely conscious of each other, and it would be a joy to see him and to hear his voice.

He was in the Drawing-Room, and as Fedora with her

father beside her entered the room, they saw he was not alone.

The Chief Constable, a tall, military-looking man, was with him.

Once they were introduced, Sir Archibald exclaimed to her father:

"Now I remember! We met once in London many years ago! I think it must have been at the opening of the Royal Academy."

"Of course!" Alexander Colwyn replied. "You asked my opinion about one of the paintings."

"And you were very rude about it!"

The two men were laughing and the Earl put a glass of champagne into Fedora's hand. As his fingers touched hers, she felt a thrill like a streak of lightning pass through her and she knew he felt the same.

Lady Sheelah appeared when everybody else was present and once again she made an entrance in another fantastic, theatrical gown.

This one was white, glittering with sequins, and her lace bertha was picked out in *diamanté*.

There were white flowers in her red hair held in place by a huge brooch of diamonds, and a diamond necklace encircled her neck.

She was charming to the Chief Constable, very possessive in her attitude towards the Earl, and she ignored Fedora as if she were invisible.

This was what Fedora preferred anyway, and although the conversation at dinner was interesting and at times sparkling, she took very little part in it.

Only when she and Lady Sheelah left the Dining-Room did she feel uncomfortable, and she thought it would be embarrassing if they were to remain in stony silence until they were joined by the gentlemen.

But to her surprise Lady Sheelah, having spent some minutes in front of the mirror, said:

"I wonder if you would do something for me, Miss Colwyn?"

"Y-yes . . . of course," Fedora replied.

"I find I have no handkerchief in my reticule," Lady Sheelah said. "Would you be very obliging and go to my bedroom to get one for me?"

Fedora was surprised, and Lady Sheelah explained:

"At this time of the evening all the servants are downstairs having their own dinner, and I do not like to disturb my maid."

"No, of course not. I will fetch it for you."

"You will find my room quite easily," Lady Sheelah said. "It is next to His Lordship's and I know that you and your father were there this morning."

Fedora was aware that this must have annoyed her, but because she was not being actively rude at the moment she was only too willing to do as she asked.

"Where will I find your handkerchiefs?" she enquired.

"In a sachet in the left-hand drawer of my dressing-table. Bring me one edged with lace."

"I will do that."

Fedora left the Drawing-Room, walked up the stairs, and moved along the wide corridor where she had been twice before when visiting the Earl's Sitting-Room.

It was a long way, and because she was sure that as the Chief Constable was there the gentlemen would not hurry from the Dining-Room, she stopped once or twice to look at the paintings her father had admired earlier in the day.

Finally, however, she saw the two painted doors ahead of her which led into the Earl's Suite, and with an unmistakable little stab at her heart she was vividly aware that the door next to the Earl's led to the room where Lady Sheelah slept.

The door was not closed, and to her surprise she saw that the room was not empty, for Lady Sheelah's maid was there.

She was pulling the curtains and turned with a little exclamation of surprise as Fedora entered the room.

"I am sorry if I startled you," Fedora said with a smile, "but Her Ladyship thought you would be downstairs having your supper, and she wants a handkerchief."

The maid, who was a middle-aged woman, replied sharply:

"I gave Her Ladyship one."

"Perhaps she has mislaid it," Fedora suggested.

"That wouldn't surprise me!" the maid said tartly.

She went to the drawer of the dressing-table, opened it, and Fedora saw inside a satin sachet such as Lady Sheelah had described.

The maid drew out a handkerchief, a small square of fine linen with a deep edging of lace.

"Here you are, Miss."

"I am glad you were here to give it to me," Fedora said. "I expect I should have chosen the wrong one!"

"I came up to shut the window," the maid said. "It's raining cats and dogs!"

"Oh, is it?" Fedora exclaimed. "I had no idea!"

"I thought the sunshine was too good to last," the maid said, "and I warned the housemaids. But they never listens, and pulls the curtains without shutting the windows!"

Fedora thought the maid was enjoying her grumble against somebody else, and moved towards the door.

As she did so, a man dressed as a valet and carrying a coat over his arm which she recognised as one belonging to the Earl said:

"Come on! Everything's all right, and your supper'll be getting cold."

He spoke before he saw Fedora, then added quickly:

"I'm sorry, Miss! I didn't notice you!"

"I came up to fetch a handkerchief for Lady Sheelah," Fedora explained, feeling she must justify her presence in the room. "She thought you would all be having your supper."

"And so we should be, Miss, except for the rain."

"They should shut the windows when they pulls the curtains!" the maid said in an aggrieved tone. "You can't trust 'em, not any of 'em!"

"That's a fact!" the valet agreed.

"Well, good-night," Fedora said. "I only hope we are not in for a thunderstorm."

As she spoke, she thought that if there was one, it was not likely to do much damage to the Castle.

But at home the roof could be damaged even more than it was already, and the rain would drive in under the tiles that needed restoring, and another ceiling would fall at Mountsorrel.

As she made her way down the passage she could hear the lady's-maid saying how much she disliked thunder and lightning and how dangerous it was for those who were out in it.

Then she forgot the servants as once again she was looking at the paintings and she paused for some time to admire a very lovely Dutch interior that had particularly pleased her father.

As she expected, when she reached the Drawing-Room there was still no sign of the gentlemen who had not yet left the Dining-Room.

Lady Sheelah, however, was seated in her favourite place on the sofa, the folds of her full skirt carefully arranged over it.

She took the handkerchief from Fedora, saying:

"You have been a long time!"

"The Castle is so big."

"Far too big for one man to live in alone!"

Fedora thought she was being deliberately provocative and did not reply.

Then before Lady Sheelah could say anything more, there was the sound of voices outside and the gentlemen came into the room.

They were laughing at something that had been said and Lord Ludlow and Sir Ian were smoking cigars.

But Fedora had eyes only for the Earl, and she thought that if there were a hundred men present, he would still be outstandingly handsome and have an aura of power and authority which she was sure derived from his character more than from his rank.

She was looking for him and he was looking for her, and for a moment their eyes met and everything vanished except their need of each other and the love that seemed to vibrate between them.

Then Lord Ludlow stood looking down at Lady Sheelah, and the Earl invited the Chief Constable to sit beside Fedora.

"You must talk to Miss Colwyn, Sir Archibald," he said. "I am sure she will wish to know what her father was like all those years ago."

"There is no need for me to say that you are very like your mother, Miss Colwyn," the Chief Constable said as he smiled at Fedora. "I remember meeting her at the Academy when I met your father, and thought she was far more beautiful than any of the paintings."

"She would have been very proud to know you thought so," Fedora replied, "and I am honoured that you should think I am like her."

"You are indeed!" the Chief Constable said. "And I must tell you . . ."

Quite suddenly the door of the Drawing-Room was flung noisily open, and as everybody's head turned instinctively to look, a woman whom Fedora recognised as one of the Nurses in attendance on the Countess rushed into the room.

She ran towards the Earl, and when she reached him she was so breathless that for the moment she could not speak.

Then, the words coming in gasps, she said:

"M'Lord! Oh, M'Lord! Quick! Come at once!"

"What is it? What has happened?" the Earl enquired.

"Her Ladyship's—oh, M'Lord—I don't know how to tell you!"

"What has happened?"

"Her Ladyship's been—murdered! Stabbed! She's—dead!"

Chapter Seven

For a moment there was a stunned silence. Then the Chief Constable got to his feet and walked towards the Earl.

The Nurse was sobbing noisily and the Earl said to her sharply:

"We will come with you, Miss Jones."

Nobody spoke as they moved towards the door, until as they reached it the Chief Constable paused and looked back to say:

"I should be grateful if everybody would stay here and not leave the room until I return."

Then he and the Earl walked out and the door closed behind them.

Sir Ian spoke first.

"This is certainly something I did not expect!" he remarked. "Who on earth could have wished to kill that poor, unfortunate woman who has been like a millstone round Kimball's neck ever since he married her?"

Even as he spoke the reply was so obvious that again there was an uncomfortable silence.

After a moment Major Gower said:

"I think it would be a mistake to speculate on what has happened until we have some evidence. The Nurse seemed to me to be very hysterical."

"Yes, very!" Lord Ludlow agreed.

As he spoke, he moved to sit down beside Lady Sheelah

131

to talk to her in a low voice which was obviously not meant to be overheard by anybody else.

Alexander Colwyn rose to his feet:

"I intend to spend the time," he said, "in looking at these paintings, and I suggest, Fedora, that you and I decide what needs to be done to them, especially the Fragonard, which in my opinion is exceptionally beautiful."

The quiet way he spoke made it easy for Fedora to reply without anybody being aware that her heart was thumping. She was thinking only of the Earl, and the suspense of waiting to hear what had occurred was unbearable.

Then as she could not help thinking that if his wife was dead he would be free of the burden he had carried for so long, she realised that he would above all things dislike a scandal.

He may have been ashamed and humiliated by having a wife who was mad, but it was even more distressing to have the world know she had been murdered.

Then as she stood in front of the Fragonard, the implication of Sir Ian's words made her suddenly afraid.

Suppose by some terrible error of judgement the Earl was accused of murdering the woman who was ruining his life?

Such an idea was ridiculous, she told herself.

For if, as she suspected, the Countess had been murdered while the Nurses were having their supper, then the Earl would have been in the Dining-Room with the other guests, and he could not possibly be suspected of having committed such a horrible crime.

But because she loved him she was apprehensive, and although her father went on talking, she had not the slightest idea what he was saying.

She was only praying frantically that there would be some quite logical explanation of the Countess's death.

After what seemed to be an interminable time, the Earl came back to the Drawing-Room.

He was looking very serious and, Fedora thought as she glanced quickly at him, rather pale.

There was silence as he walked slowly down the room to stand with his back to the mantelpiece, and it was obvious that he had something important to say.

Lady Sheelah, seated beside Lord Ludlow, looked up at him, while Sir Ian and Major Gower, who had been standing talking on the other side of the room, moved near, as did Fedora and her father.

Nobody spoke, and after a moment the Earl said:

"I am afraid what I have to tell you is very serious. The two Nurses had given my wife a sleeping-draught and she was asleep when they left her bedroom to go down-stairs for their supper. They locked the door of the Suite from the outside and left the key in the lock. While they were away, and it was less than an hour, somebody entered my wife's room and stabbed her through the heart . . ."

There was a pause. Then the Earl went on:

"With an artist's palette-knife!"

There was an audible gasp and everybody's eyes turned towards Alexander Colwyn.

"Was it one of my knives from the Studio?" he asked.

The Earl nodded.

"I suppose it would be quite easy for somebody . . ." Alexander Colwyn began.

But before he had said more than a few words, Lady Sheelah gave a little laugh.

"Surely," she said, "that solves your problem very easily? There is your murderess!"

She pointed, her diamond bracelets glittering as she did so, at Fedora.

Again there was a gasp of astonishment, and before Fedora could find her voice Lady Sheelah went on:

"Miss Colwyn left me after dinner and was away for a long time. In fact she only returned here just before you gentlemen came from the Dining-Room."

"Where did you go?"

The Earl asked the question in a voice that did not sound like his own.

Fedora, feeling as if she had stepped into a nightmare, replied:

"At her Ladyship's request, I went to her bedroom to fetch her a handkerchief which she said she had forgotten."

Lady Sheelah laughed again.

"A likely story! My maid always provides me with a handkerchief, and I certainly did not need another one."

Fedora felt she could not have heard her aright.

Then as she stared at her incredulously, suddenly vividly aware of what Lady Sheelah was trying to do, she found herself saying almost as if somebody prompted her:

"That is what your lady's-maid said when she gave me the handkerchief I brought downstairs to you."

She saw Lady Sheelah's eyes widen. Then before she could speak the Earl said:

"When you went to Lady Sheelah's bedroom for the handkerchief, you say her maid was there?"

"Yes," Fedora answered. "She was closing the windows because it was raining, and Your Lordship's valet had been doing the same in your room."

She met the Earl's eyes as she spoke, and she felt as if he put out his arms towards her and held her close to protect her.

"That makes it quite easy to establish where you were," he said quietly, "and I will go and inform the Chief Constable of what has been said. He is at the moment talking to the Nurses."

Without looking at anybody else in the room except Fedora, he walked towards the door. Only when he shut it behind him and the house-party was once again left alone did Sir Ian say drily:

"It seems extraordinary, Sheelah, that you should have forgotten that you had asked Miss Colwyn to fetch you a handkerchief!"

It was then that Fedora was aware that Lady Sheelah was looking very pale and the faint patches of rouge on her cheeks stood out in a strange manner.

Before anyone else could speak, Lord Ludlow rose and drew her to her feet.

"Come," he said.

"Where to?" she asked, and there was a frightened note in her voice.

"I am taking you to France."

"No—what do you—mean?"

"Do not be—stupid!" he said. "If you stay here they will hang you."

Lady Sheelah gave a cry of horror and he went on:

"If we drive straight to Dover we can be across the Channel long before there is a warrant out for your arrest."

As he was speaking he was drawing her towards the door while everybody else in the room watched them as if paralysed.

For a moment Lady Sheelah appeared to resist him. Then she said:

"My jewels! My jewels! I cannot leave without my jewels!"

"I will buy you more," Lord Ludlow replied. "Have you forgotten that the Chief Constable is in the house? When he returns here, having heard the evidence of your maid and Kimball's valet, there will be no further chance of escape."

Lady Sheelah made a little murmur, then without another word she allowed Lord Ludlow to lead her from the room.

Only when they had left did Fedora sit down suddenly as if she might faint.

As if he was aware what she was feeling, Sir Ian went to the table in a corner of the room to pour out a small glass of brandy, and as he was doing so Major Gower exclaimed:

"My God! When I said that Sheelah would fight like a tiger to keep Kimball, I did not realise she would commit murder!"

"And try to implicate my daughter in the process," Alexander Colwyn said angrily.

Sir Ian handed the glass of brandy to Fedora.

"I ... I am all ... right," she tried to say.

At the same time, she felt as if her head was swimming and there was a darkness coming up from the floor.

135

Then as Sir Ian guided her hand, holding the glass to her lips, she felt the fiery liquid seep down her throat.

"I think we all need a drink!" Major Gower exclaimed. "What will you have, Sir?"

He spoke to Alexander Colwyn, who answered:

"A brandy, please."

He rose from the chair in which he was sitting and walked towards Major Gower.

Fedora, looking up at Sir Ian, asked in a whisper:

"Will they . . . get . . . away?"

"I expect so," he replied. "Ludlow has a team of excellent horses, and by the time the Chief Constable understands what really happened, they should be out of his jurisdiction and will be in France before a warrant can be issued for Lady Sheelah's arrest."

"H-how could . . . she have . . . done such a . . . thing?"

"I think she realised that our host's interest had turned elsewhere."

The way he spoke made Fedora aware that he, at any rate, had guessed what she and the Earl felt for each other.

It was not surprising, for she knew, just as she had seen from the expression in his eyes what Lord Ludlow felt for Lady Sheelah, that it would have been obvious to anyone who was at all perceptive what she and the Earl felt for each other.

But that still left him involved in a scandal, and she longed to comfort him in what she knew was an ordeal which would be painful and humiliating.

"I love him!" she told herself. "And only . . . love can help him . . . now."

* * *

Fedora arranged a great bowl of pink roses in the Sitting-Room and felt that their loveliness and the fragrance somehow compensated for the threadbare carpet and the tattered curtains.

Their colour echoed the glowing hues of the paintings

on the wall, but she was sure that the Earl, when he arrived, would notice little except herself.

She and her father had come home over two weeks ago, but it seemed like centuries.

Yet, at the same time, a wonderful happiness had replaced the despair and misery she had felt when the Earl had told her of his love but that they must part.

Sometimes she felt as if she had dreamt the drama at the Castle and also the love she had found there.

Then again she would know it was very real and that God in His mercy had answered her prayers and the Earl was free.

Even now she found it difficult to believe that Lady Sheelah had actually stooped to committing murder so as to keep the Earl when she thought she was losing him, and planning to eliminate at the same time not only his wife but Fedora herself.

It had been a clever plot, and had it not been for the shower of rain, she might at this moment be awaiting trial for murder.

Because Lady Sheelah's bedroom was further from the Drawing-Room than the Countess's, Lady Sheelah had plenty of time, while Fedora was fetching her handkerchief, to slip up the side-staircase which led to the tower.

She must have collected the palette-knife from the Studio, entered the Countess's bedroom where she lay in a drugged sleep, and stabbed her through the heart.

She then returned to the Drawing-Room without being seen by anybody.

Fedora had not only stopped to talk with the maid and the Earl's valet, but also had lingered to admire the paintings in the corridor, having no wish to be alone with Lady Sheelah before they were joined by the gentlemen from the Dining-Room.

Sometimes in the night she would wake up and say a prayer of gratitude that fate, or perhaps her mother, had given her such an indisputable alibi and despite the fact that the death had been caused by a palette-knife, it was impossible for her to be implicated.

She thought too that it had been extremely fortunate that Lord Ludlow, who desired Lady Sheelah for himself, had been there and ready to take her away.

It had been quite a long time after they had gone before the Chief Constable and the Earl returned to the Drawing-Room.

They were both looking very serious, and because Fedora loved the Earl she was aware of how uncomfortable he was feeling in the knowledge that it was to free him for herself that Lady Sheelah had committed such a terrible crime.

"I said that nobody was to leave the room," the Chief Constable said sharply when he saw that there were only four people waiting for him instead of six.

"Lady Sheelah was not unnaturally disturbed," Sir Ian replied.

"I regret that I must ask her to return here," the Chief Constable said.

He looked at the Earl.

"Perhaps, My Lord, you would send for her?"

The Earl hesitated.

"I imagine the servants are upset," he replied, "so perhaps it would be best if I went myself."

"Yes, if you wish," the Chief Constable agreed.

"Would you like something to drink?" Sir Ian asked, taking upon himself the role of host.

"Thank you, but I must decline until this unpleasant business is over."

"As you wish," Sir Ian answered. "And I agree it is very unpleasant."

There was an uncomfortable silence until the Chief Constable said:

"It is something I would not have expected to happen in this house, and I was very fond of Kimball's father."

"And we are very fond of his son," Major Gower said. "I hope, Sir, you will as far as possible keep the details of this tragedy out of the hands of the Press?"

"I shall certainly do what I can," the Chief Constable agreed, "but it may not be easy."

Fedora knew as he spoke that he was thinking that a crime committed by a beautiful woman like Lady Sheelah because she wished to marry the husband of the woman she had killed would certainly make headlines.

What was more, she was sure that everybody else in the room was thinking the same thing.

Nearly a quarter-of-an-hour passed before the Earl returned.

"I apologise for being so long," he said, "but there is no sign of Lady Sheelah. She has not been to her bed-room, and as far as I can ascertain she is nowhere in the Castle."

He looked at Sir Ian as he said:

"Have any of you any idea where Ludlow might have taken her? As it is raining, I cannot imagine they would be outside in the garden."

Sir Ian did not answer, and Fedora knew he was con-sidering whether he should tell the truth, and whether enough time had elapsed for Lady Sheelah and Lord Ludlow to have got away.

She thought that even allowing for the saddling of the horses they must have covered some distance by now, and Sir Ian obviously thought the same thing.

"I hope," he said to the Chief Constable, "in your private capacity you will be prepared to admit that Lord Ludlow has done the right thing in taking Lady Sheelah, for whom he has always had a fondness, out of reach of the law."

For a moment the Chief Constable looked startled. Then he said quietly:

"Unofficially, I agree with you."

* * *

They had all left early the next morning, and Fe-dora and her father drove away from the Castle in a very different manner from that in which they had ar-rived.

The Earl's travelling-chariot, drawn by four superla-tive horses, took them to London.

The chariot was so well sprung and so comfortable that her father declared he was not in the least tired.

They stopped at an Inn for luncheon on the way and found that the Earl had provided not only most of the food but also a fine claret and a vintage brandy which sustained Alexander Colwyn on the journey.

When they reached London they stayed at Heversham House in Grosvenor Square, and although her father retired to bed at once, Fedora was entranced by the treasures that the Earl's town-house contained.

There were a number of paintings that she knew would thrill her father when he was not too exhausted to enjoy them.

The Comptroller who met them on their arrival informed her what had been arranged.

"His Lordship has written to me, Miss Colwyn," he said, "and is most insistent that you should stay two nights so that your father will not be over-tired by the long journey home."

"That is very kind," Fedora murmured.

"His Lordship has also asked me to arrange for a dressmaker to call, and I wondered if tomorrow morning at ten o'clock would suit you."

"A dressmaker?"

The Comptroller looked puzzled.

"I thought you would know about it, Miss Colwyn. His Lordship writes that he has arranged for you to be painted with the pink water-lilies which his mother planted in the fountain of the French flower-garden at the Castle."

He saw by the expression on Fedora's face that she remembered that this was what the Earl had said he wanted. Yet she had thought at the time that it was something which would never happen.

"His Lordship," the Comptroller went on, "is very insistent that the colour of the gown you wear for the portrait should be exactly the same as the robe of the Madonna in the Van Dyck that hangs in his private Sitting-Room."

He produced a piece of silk which he held out for Fedora's inspection.

"This is the colour that His Lordship insists is the right one, subject of course to your approval. And he suggests, Miss Colwyn, that your father should advise him as to which artist should be commissioned to paint the portrait in question, and that meanwhile you order two gowns immediately, one for the afternoon, in case that is the more suitable, and one for the evening."

Fedora smiled.

She appreciated the way in which the Earl had been clever enough to provide her with the gowns she needed without infringing on the conventions and to make it easy for her to accept them.

In fact, it would be impossible for her to refuse.

"Ten o'clock would suit me admirably," she replied.

On the following day they had set off, again in the Earl's travelling-chariot.

Her father could talk of nothing but the paintings at Heversham House, while Jim was bubbling over as he whispered to her of the food and wine they were taking home with them.

"There'll be no question of th' Master slipping back ter th' condition 'e were in when we left, Miss Fedora," he said gleefully. "In fact we'll 'ave ter eat like 'orses if we don't want t' waste a lot o' good victuals."

"We certainly do not want to do that, Jim," Fedora agreed.

She longed to thank the Earl personally and tell him how wonderful it was of him to see to every detail for their comfort.

'Could any man be so marvellous,' she thought, 'when he has so much to think about at the moment and so many worries?'

She knew that their love linked them together, and that was inviolate, whatever else occurred.

She felt as if everything were enveloped with the love that the Earl radiated towards her and which she knew,

141

because it was joined with faith and hope, she in her turn radiated towards everyone else.

Even Mountsorrel looked less dilapidated than it had when she had left it, and as if fate had suddenly decided she had suffered enough and the future was golden, there was a letter in the Hall, which had been pushed through the letter-box in their absence.

Fedora picked it up with a leap of her heart because she knew it was from Philip.

She thought perhaps it was to say that he was coming home.

Then when she opened the envelope she found inside a cheque made out to her father, and stared at it incredulously.

Hastily she read the letter.

My Dearest Fedora,

You must forgive me if I have been somewhat tardy in writing these last few months, but I have not had a minute to myself.

Everything I hoped for has suddenly begun to materialise, and unless anything unforeseen occurs, I hope in two or three years to come home to you an exceedingly rich man.

In the meantime, I am sending you a cheque for one hundred pounds and will follow it with the same amount every month until, as I hope, I will be able perhaps to double or even treble it.

I knew, my dearest Sister, how worried you must have been about money when I received your letter saying that Papa was not well, but this, I hope, will make a lot of difference. I promise you that when I do come home, your devotion and unselfishness these past years will not go unrewarded.

Give Papa my love and tell him I shall be very disappointed if he does not look as well cared for as our paintings.

Thank you again, my dearest Fedora,

Your grateful and affectionate brother
Philip

"He has sent Papa a hundred pounds!"

Fedora could hardly believe it, but she knew now that they could immediately pay back their debt to Mr. Lewenstein and live in a very different way from what they had done before.

She realised that while she had been reading the letter, Jim had taken her father upstairs to his bedroom, and she ran after them, bursting in to tell them both the good news.

There was a great deal for her to do at home, and while Jim whistled at his work, her father was busy on the Poussin, which, to her surprise, Fedora found had travelled with them. Meanwhile, she knew that she was waiting, longing and praying for news from the Castle.

Every day she scanned the newspapers, which they could now afford to buy, afraid she would read a report of the murder of the Countess of Heversham.

Instead there was only a formal notice in the Obituary-Column stating that the wife of the Earl had been interred in the family vault and the Service had been a private one.

"What is happening? I must know what is happening!" Fedora would say a dozen times a day, and tried to console herself with the old adage that "No news is good news."

Her new gowns, expensive and very fashionable, arrived from London, and when she tried them on she knew that the colour was exactly the shade of pink chosen by Van Dyck for the Madonna.

It made her skin look dazzlingly white, and with her dark hair parted in the middle and her eyes bright with hope, it was easy to see her resemblance to the painting hanging in her bedroom.

She had put on her day-gown today in the faint but irrepressible hope that the Earl might be able to come to her, even though she told herself it was extremely unlikely.

With Philip's money she had purchased some of the other things she required so urgently, and although she felt it was perhaps an extravagance, she had ordered a new riding-habit.

She told herself humbly that she was being presumptuous in thinking what she was too frightened to put into words even to herself. Yet, an instinct stronger than logic made her feel that the Earl needed her as she so desperately needed him.

As she stood back to admire the roses in a bowl on the table and knew that they blended with the silk of her gown, she thought she heard the sound of wheels outside the front door, and she held her breath.

Then she told herself it had just been the rustle of her very full skirts and the silk petticoats trimmed with lace that went underneath.

Yet she was certain, almost certain, that she heard the jingle of a horse's bridle and footsteps which made her feel as if her heart were moving from her breast into her throat.

She did not move, for it was impossible to do so.

The front door had been left open to the sunshine and the footsteps were coming across the Hall towards the Sitting-Room.

Suddenly he was there.

He seemed to fill the whole room, the sky, and the world itself, and she knew as she saw his eyes that he looked younger and happier and completely different from the man she had left behind.

Neither of them could speak, they just stood looking at each other. Then the Earl opened his arms and with a little cry that seemed to echo round the room Fedora ran towards him.

He held her close against him and she could feel his heart beating frantically against her breast.

Then he turned her face up to his and looked down at her before his lips were on hers.

He kissed her until the whole room swung round them, and they no longer had their feet on the ground but were flying towards the Heaven they had sought before and lost.

"I love you!" the Earl said at last, and his voice was hoarse and unsteady. "I love you, my darling, and thank God I am no longer afraid to say so! I love you! I love you!"

Then he was kissing her again, kissing her passionately, possessively, demandingly, as if they had both survived inexpressible dangers and had been saved by a miracle.

Now there was only love, a love so radiant, so dazzling that it blinded them, and there were no words in which to describe it.

* * *

A very long time later, the Earl said, his voice still hoarse, unsteady, and very unlike his own:

"Let me look at you, my precious one. I still find it hard to believe you are real and that for the rest of my life I need not have to be content to look only at your picture."

"I . . . I am . . . wearing the gown which you . . . gave me . . . because I . . . I thought you might come today."

As she spoke, he held her close against him and traced with the first finger of his right hand her two winged eye-brows. Then he ran it down her straight little nose and finally outlined her soft curved mouth.

It gave her a strangely exciting feeling which made her first draw in her breath, and then it came fitfully through her lips while her breasts moved as if to music.

"I am drawing a picture of love," the Earl said tenderly. "Does it excite you, my darling?"

"I . . . love . . . you!"

The words were almost inaudible, but there was a note of passion in them and it made the Earl kiss her again.

"You are mine," he said at length, "and nothing else matters. It has been an agony to have to wait for so long, but you understand there was a great deal I had to see to."

"What . . . happened?"

145

Fedora found it difficult to ask the question in case things were worse than she had feared.

"That is what I want to tell you," he replied, "but for the moment I can only think how beautiful you are and that nothing else is of the least importance."

"That is . . . what I feel," she answered, "but . . . please . . . I must know."

"Yes, of course, my precious," he replied.

He drew her towards the sofa and as he sat down she said:

- "B-but you have been travelling . . . you need a drink. Is there . . . anything I can get you?"

"No, nothing," he replied. "How can you be so perfect, so exquisite, so uncannily like my Madonna, the one I have worshipped ever since I was a child?"

He took her hand, kissed her fingers, then said:

"I am trying to think what I ought to tell you, but all I want to do is to go on saying how much I love you."

"Tell me," Fedora said. "Then perhaps we . . . need not . . . speak of it . . . again."

There was just a little tremble in her voice as she thought that he might tell her that Lady Sheelah had somehow been forced to come back from France in order to stand trial for murder. Then he said:

"The Chief Constable has been marvellous! There was of course an inquest, but he managed to ensure that the verdict was 'Death by misadventure.' "

Fedora gave a little cry.

"Is that true . . . really true?"

"As the Police could not find anybody to testify that they had seen the murderer, nor was there anybody who could reasonably be apprehended as a suspect, the whole case has been dropped."

Fedora gave a deep sigh.

"I have been so . . . worried for . . . you."

"And I was worried, my darling, in case it should hurt you," the Earl replied. "I had no wish for you to be

involved, even as a guest in the Castle, in anything so—
unsavoury."

His voice deepened on the last word and Fedora thought
that it contained all the pain and unhappiness that he
had suffered for so many years.

Then he added:

"Now it is all over and I am free, my lovely—free to
ask you if you will marry me and give me the happiness
which I have never had."

"That is what I . . . want to do," Fedora replied. "And I
want to make you . . . forget."

"That will be easy, once I have you beside me," he
said, "and, my sweet, I have been thinking while driving
here that it would be intolerable for both of us to have to
wait for the conventional year of mourning."

He saw Fedora's eyes lighten as if the sunshine was
caught in them, before she said:

"Do you mean . . . could it be . . . possible . . . ?"

"If you agree," the Earl said, "we will have a very
quiet and secret marriage. Then I thought we could go
away to one of my other houses. I have one which is very
beautiful and rather isolated in the wilds of Devon. When
it is accepted that my time of mourning is over, we can
announce that we have been married there—that is, if
you agree."

Fedora made an inarticulate little sound of happiness,
and there was no need for her to say any more.

"What I thought," the Earl went on, "is that we could
ask your father to live in the Castle in our absence and
work on the paintings. He will be very well looked after,
and as I am certain there are a number of my relatives
who will wish not only to call at the Castle but to stay
there, he will not be alone."

"How can you . . . think of such wonderful . . . perfect
things?" Fedora asked. "And you . . . know I want to
be . . . with you."

"I cannot tell you how much I want it too, and that I
cannot live without you," the Earl replied. "As I had the

feeling you might agree, I already have a Special Licence with me!"

He put his arms round her and drew her closer to him. Then he asked:

"Will you marry me, my beautiful Madonna, who are already in a shrine in my heart, and whom I will adore and worship for the rest of my life?"

He did not wait for her to say "yes" because his lips were on hers, and he knew as she seemed to melt into him that their closeness made them not two people but one.

ABOUT THE AUTHOR

BARBARA CARTLAND, the world's most famous romantic novelist, who is also an historian, playwright, lecturer, political speaker and television personality, has now written over 300 books.

She has also had many historical works published and has written four autobiographies as well as the biographies of her mother and that of her brother Ronald Cartland, who was the first Member of Parliament to be killed in W.W. II. This book has a preface by Sir Winston Churchill and has just been republished with an introduction by Sir Arthur Bryant.

Barbara Cartland has sold 200 million books over the world, more than half of these in the U.S.A. She broke the world record in 1975 by writing twenty-three books and the four subsequent years with 20, 21, 23 and 24. In addition her album of love songs has just been published, sung with the Royal Philharmonic Orchestra.

Barbara Cartland, who is a Dame of the Order of St. John of Jerusalem, has championed the cause for old people and founded the first Romany Gypsy Camp in the world.

Barbara Cartland is deeply interested in Vitamin Therapy and is President of the British National Association for Health. Her book the *Magic of Honey* has sold in millions all over the world

She has a magazine *The World of Romance* and her Barbara Cartland Romantic World Tours will, in conjunction with British Airways, carry travelers to England, Egypt, India, France, Germany and Turkey.